2006 Writer's Blog Anthology

A Collection of Works by Writers Who Blog

Edited by Deborah Woehr

First Edition September 2006

ISBN Number 978-1-4303-0929-1

Acknowledgments

Although this book has my name on the title page, it would be unforgivable for me to release it without paying proper tribute to all of the people who contributed to it. It would have been impossible to compile this book without the helpful suggestions and insights of the authors and those outside of this project.

Special thanks goes to Lee Pletzers of *Twisted Visions of an Inkslinger's Mind,* editor of six anthologies. Lee gave me some very helpful tips, which I am grateful for. My gratitude extends to John of *Syntagma Media* (partner of the Writer's Blog Alliance), Clive Allen of *Gone Away,* and Melly of *All Kinds of Writing,* Ned of *Nedful Things,* and Michael of *Smoke & Mirrors* for their invaluable critiques of this collection.

Thanks for everything.

Deborah Woehr

Introduction

Dear Reader,

What you hold in your hands is a unique collection of works by a talented group of writers, who happen to blog. You haven't heard of most, or any, of them. But they are part of a growing number of writers who use blogs as a way to build their readership.

The 2006 Writer's Blog Anthology started as a collaborative effort by the members of the *Writer's Blog Alliance*, which was co-founded by myself and Clive Allen in August of 2005, and branched out to include military blogs and other writers outside of our network. This is a multi-genre collection, composed entirely of blog posts and reader responses.

It is our hope that when you finish reading this book, you will feel compelled to visit our sites and take part in the discussions we have with our readers. We would feel honored to have you with us.

Warm regards,

Deborah Woehr
Editor, Writer's Blog Anthology
Co-founder of the Writer's Blog Alliance

Table of Contents

Marti Lawrence
Enter the Laughter

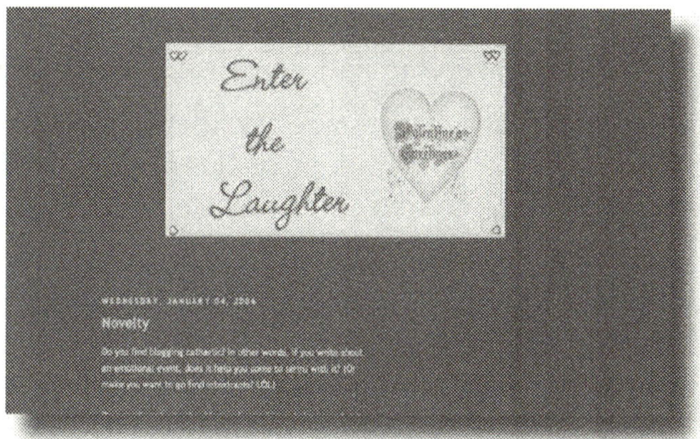

Marti Lawrence is a freelance humor columnist, published in *The Examiner Newspaper*. She has published her first novel, *Queen Klutz*, which is available at Lulu.com. Her second novel, *River of Possibilities*, will be available soon.

Novelty

Do you find blogging cathartic? In other words, if you write about an emotional event, does it help you come to terms with it? (Or make you want to go find intoxicants?)

Does reading about other bloggers' experiences help you sort out your own problems / hangups / let-downs / worries? (Or make you want to go find intoxicants?)

I know a LOT of you bloggers are writing a novel (individually of course...it's not like there is a giant room somewhere that a bunch of bloggers gather in, and attempt to produce a manuscript, although that might be pretty funny)

So tell me, when you are writing a sad, depressing, or angry scene, do you get sad / angry / depressed?

It's necessary to get into the mind of your fictional character to effectively write their words and actions, and I find myself getting caught up in it.

I am at a point in my unfinished novel where my main character has been betrayed, and I tell ya, I am paranoid about everything now. I look at the grocery clerks suspiciously, wondering if they are out to somehow stab me in the back!

So tell me (please please please please please) does this happen to other writers? Does writing your novel affect your blogging, or vice versa?

Readers Response

Uisce said, "I didn't do any *real* blogging while I was writing my novel. I wrote some posts (hidden, viewable by a select few) to let folks know how it was coming along. But the blogging didn't really intersect with the novel writing.

"Now as for getting into characters, I think that's the most interesting part of writing a novel. I have a character who had to be careful about touching other people. It's a long story, and if you want to read my novel... oh wait, I have to post it somewhere. Anyway, the point is that I found myself feeling anxious about touching other people, the way this character would have. And all the time I found myself wrapped up emotionally in what was going on with these characters. But the most amazing thing about writing a novel was that the story just wrote itself. I was just watching it happen and doing my best to capture it all.

"Now mind you, I don't know if it's any good. I don't trust my wife to give me an honest opinion and I don't think anyone else has read it all the way through. Well I've rambled enough! What was the question? Oh yeah, what you're going through is totally normal. I think you just need to write some short stories about someone who was really paranoid and was visited by a magic fairy who blew pixie dust and made it all go away."

threecollie said, "I think blogging certainly helps the writing process. Although my only novel was written years ago (only written, not published) I think the limitations of space and attention span on a blog have helped me do a better job with my newspaper column. Of course, this could just be wishful thinking. I do think though that if you have reached the point where your characters have become real enough that you can identify them, then you are doing a good job developing them and making them real for your readers as well."

cube said, "For me, blogging is different from writing. I don't blog about personal events. I like to keep my blogging satirical, but that's just me."

Chas said, "I am writing a novel now but its stuck on Chapter 3. But its not blogging that halted the creative juices. It's more like I need a friggin inspiration probably a romantic one. And regarding to blogging I just love doing it since I am a big show off as well so it works perfectly."

FTS said, "Absolutely. Sometimes blogging helps get the creative juices flowing. I don't typically spew much venom, and when I feel the need I now use my working journal, which the public cannot see. I'm almost always glad I didn't publish the posts I write in there. Although I enjoy all of my reads, I am particularly fond of the more humorous bloggers."

Jamie Dawn said, "I'm not writing any novels, books, or anything for submission of any kind. I just write on my blog out of a love of writing. I have enjoyed writing since I was little. I love reading the comments on my blog and reading the posts of fellow bloggers. I don't like reading blogs that are really serious or drone on about boring details. I enjoy shorter posts with humor."

Wil said, "I replied over at Snoozelets."

puremood said, "No novels for me but writing on my blog can be good therapy, if need be. I don't rant much or anything but sometimes it just feels good to say something...."

zazzafooky said, "A good outlet. That about sums it up for me in the simplest way. It's not exactly therapeutic nor a spiritual necessity, more like a little route to somewhere else."

Marti said, "Thank you all for stopping by. I'm still struggling with this, I've cut back to just writing a few really depressing paragraphs and then doing something else. I really appreciate hearing other takes on this, thank you so much.

Slittin' on the Dock of Ebay

I make a little money selling stuff at E-Bay, and most of the time it's a lot of fun.

Christmas can get a wee bit crazy though, and I am about ready to slit my wrists.

Just kidding.

I do not want to speak unkindly of the buyers, because they are sweet people who send me money.

E-Bay itself, as a company, could make things just a little bit easier, though. Yo, Meg! (Margaret C. Whitman, CEO of Ebay Inc.) Have you ever tried to list anything yourself? Here, have a Prozac and we'll run through it together.

Let's list this Christmas ornament. No, Meg, we're not going to worry about political correctness and call it a Holiday Ornament. It's a Santa Claus for Christ's sake. No I'm not cursing at you; Christmas *is* for Christ's sake.

Let's have a shot of whiskey.

OK, here's the home page. What's with this "it" thing?

(Meg shrugs)

Now we'll go to "Sell". Oh, I see somebody else complained, 'cause you've got a new version of the ***Sell Your Item*** form.

'Bout friggin' time, Meg.

Allrighty. . .what's this? Take a survey? I don't think so hon, we've got to move these refrigerators, gotta sell these color TV's.

Don't look at me like that Meg, it's a joke. I know we're selling an ornament. Don't you remember the rock video for "Money for Nothing" by Dire Straits?

(I imitate Dire Straits, playing air guitar while singing, "Money for nothin' and your chicks for free")

(Meg reaches for the whiskey bottle.)

So, it says enter a word to describe your item. I'll type in Christmas Ornament. Geez Meg, twenty categories? What if I don't KNOW what year it was made? I got it at a garage sale for cryin' out loud. Here's one that says Santa; we'll go with that.

Add a picture...sure. Edit picture. Let's see - ACK! Santa looks like a Ku Klux Klan member! Crimeny, Meg, that brightness setting is intense, huh? That's not good. Undo, undo.

Enter description. Now we're gettin' somewhere. I wrote it all up in Word, we'll just paste it in. HEY! WTF, Meg? I had it all set up with different font sizes and colors, so it'd look festive.

Now everything is the same size and color. I'm gonna have to use that gawd-awful interface to change it to the way I want. Here, we'll click on change font color and go warm up a cinnamon roll, maybe it'll be done by the time we get back.

(Several minutes later) Oh look Meg! It finally changed it to what I told it to do in the first place. You've got crumbs on your blouse. Don't blame me. Yes I'm sure it was expensive. Yes, real silk feels wonderful. I usually wear sweats, don't rub it in. Let's just get on with it, and set the price and shipping.

Now we'll preview it. Ah oh. It's mangled, Meg. The description is all over the place. Some of it is centered, some isn't. Put the bottle down and look. Why is it showing a gift icon? I didn't click that...hey that costs an extra quarter!

(Removes gift icon, frowns severely at Meg, who is looking away while softly whistling a tune that sounds like, "I can't imagine how that extra charge thingy got there, and damn you for noticing")

I sigh. We're almost done. What's that? No, I don't want to pay $20 to make it a featured item. It's selling for a dollar, Meg. A dollar. We're going to submit it now.

Let's do this Meg; let's push the button together, and then we'll have another drink.

(A mushroom cloud rises somewhere in the world, as Meg and I raise our glasses.)

Readers Response

Chickadee said, "(Laughing my ass off)....Ohhhh that is too funny. My husband has recently been bitten by the eBay bug. As a seller, I haven't heard too many complaints from him. As a buyer, now that's a different story..."

lee pletzers said, "I enjoyed that! Nice post, and got the point across clearly."

Anonymous said, "Oh, Marti! As usual, your witty writing is cracking me up! That was very entertaining! And in the immortal words of Dennis Leary 'Merry F'ing Christmas'! (these weren't the ACTUAL immortal of Dennis as I didn't want to offend your comment section guests) But, yeah, I've been saying that often under my breath lately when someone cuts in line at the store or slams on their brakes in front of me or my work associate asks me if I can work some 10 hour days the next couple of weeks. 'Tis the season!"

Jean-Luc Picard said, "I've bought & sold a few things on EBay. The first time is always the trickiest."

Deborah said, "Great post, Marti. Having sold a few things on Ebay, I can totally relate."

Last Girl On Earth said, "What a great post, Marti! I used to do a tiny bit of selling on Ebay. But for all of the reasons you just gave... I GAVE UP! It seemed like I was spending WAY too much time for very little return. More power to 'ya! (So what else are you selling?)"

Rocky said, "Very funny EBay post, Marti. Glad your humor helps you through the frustration of it all."

booklover said, "I loved this post! I've sold some things on E-Bay, and it can be a pain in the a**. It's better the more you do it, but still, I wouldn't complain if some things were made easier."

Carly said, "Sounds like Meg needs to smarten up..."

Marti said, "Sorry for not responding sooner, been so danged busy with... well, you read it!

"I deeply appreciate everyone stopping by and taking time to comment. I have a link to my E-Bay auctions in the sidebar, and the little pictures are links to auctions. It's been a busy but exciting selling season. I thank all of you who've taken a peek at the goods, and love you dearly if you've actually purchased something.

"Merry Christmas to all!"

Michael Murphy
Smoke & Mirrors

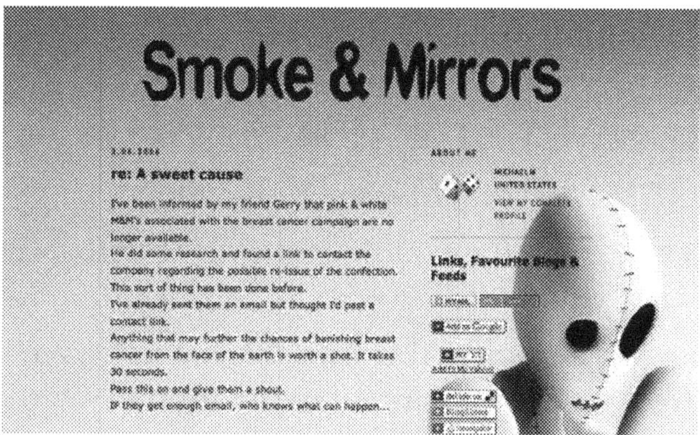

I've been blogging since February of this year but have been writing for close to ten. I began writing in the mid-nineties in an effort to cope with a mother who'd been diagnosed with Alzheimer's. A year or two later my dad was given the same diagnosis. Needless to say, I was desperate for an outlet for all the anger and pain I was experiencing and the writing just seemed to work for me.

Two pieces have been published in *The Sun,* a literary magazine out of North Carolina. I've also had several essay type pieces published in a variety of local rags. I entered an online contest in January of 2002. My piece entitled, *The Goodbye House,* won. For a little more info, go to *9TEEN,* which is my band's website.

14 Signs You May Be Suffering from BCD

#14) You know what the phrase "I got *Dooced* today" means.

#13) You are proud of the fact that you can use conditional tags.

#12) You know what 'HTML' stands for.

#11) *WWJKD*? (What would Jason Kottke do?)

#10) You wake up in the middle of the night with a sudden urge to "ping" your *blog*.

#9) You've flirted with the idea of having your *URL* permanently tattooed on your forehead. (don't laugh, it will happen, not to me but)

#8) You know what a *URL* is and you're not afraid to use one.

#7) You experience "*blog* envy" on a daily basis (sometimes hourly)

#6) You love *Technorati*. You hate Technorati. (repeat Ad Nauseum)

#5) The phrase "I have a *blog*, 'ya know," finds its way into the most mundane conversations.

#4) You utter, "I am sooo blogging that!" when any catastrophe happens, personal or otherwise, ex., a tree falls and shatters your car windshield. A post on your *blog* let's readers feel your pain. (~thanks to Lisa S at the *Truth Hurts* for the inspiration for this one)

#3) New unbridled enthusiasm reading daily email hoping the content may be *groundbreaking* fodder for a new original post.

#2) You know that the *Martian Anthropologist* isn't really an alien at all, or is he? He sure posts a lot for a human . . .

#1) You keep repeating, "*CSS* is my friend, CSS is my friend."

Readers Response

Sherri said, "OMG! This was so funny! Great post!"

JMB said, "(Laugh out loud) I can relate to that!"

Anonymous said, "Ok, I need help, lol."

Le laquet said," Excellent post."

tj at fitness.com said, "So true this post. Number 5 and 10 rang so true for me... scary stuff"

Beau said, "Clever and funny post. I hope there is treatment for BCD, as I imagine many bloggers fall into that category."

Martian Anthropologist said, "I'm flattered to have made your list! As a matter of fact, either tomorrow or Tuesday, the truth will FINALLY be blogged on my site about whether I'm really an alien or not. Or will it?"

Teh Blogfather said, "(Laugh out loud), how very true."

MarkD60 said, "I check my blog for comments before checking my email."

lisa schamess said, "I'm more likely to indulge in 5 than 4, but thanks for the plug!"

InterstellarLass said, "My real life is over...give me all blogging all the time!"

Carnealian said, "Apparently I'm just a poser blogger. None of this makes sense!"

Kathryn Beach said, "The Martian Anthropologist made me come here and read this."

The Editors said, "I'm not that far gone yet, apparently, because I can only relate to the signs 1-5. I got your email but can't see your comment on my site, where I need it so everyone can think I'm popular and cool. I laughed at the RESTROOM sign but when I clicked nothing happened. Guess I'll have to use my own."

Larissa Archer
Writhing in Apathy

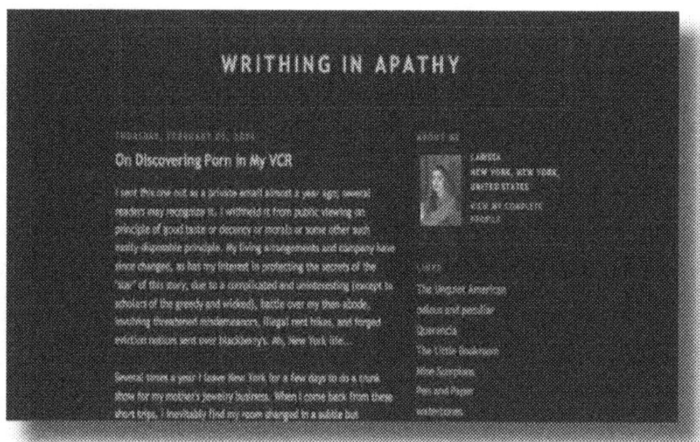

I write for *New York Moves* magazine and am a theatre actress. I'm originally from San Francisco, and I studied the "Great Books" at St. John's College in Santa Fe, NM. My blog, *Writhing in Apathy,* is mostly about the horrors of existence, such as cockroaches, bad jobs, snot, good cake, celebrities, bra shopping, and ancient history.

Cockroach Shock and Awe Part Two: Beyond Therapy

July 3rd, 2005: At 7:10 this morning I was enjoying the sleep of the innocent when I felt something tickle my knee. The sensation did not resemble the occasional trickle of sweat I ignore these sultry nights without air conditioning; it was definitely heavier, and was moving up rather than down my leg or over the side—it seemed to have a deliberate path and not the random meandering of a bead of liquid. An inner alarm roused me.

In the dim, it appeared to my bleary eyes that my cell phone had sprouted legs and embarked on an early morning hike, but I quickly realized that my new bedfellow was in fact the largest cockroach I have ever seen. I shrieked and knocked it off my leg and kicked my sheet to the floor. Suddenly awake and full of horror, I hoped against hope that the last thirty seconds had been a hideously vivid nightmare, so I gingerly picked the sheet up off the floor to prove to myself that the beast was real.

I found nothing under the blanket, and, thus relieved, might have believed the truth to be a dream and returned to rest, assured in my delusion that life was still beautiful; however, the brown mass clumsily scaling the side of my mattress robbed me forever of such peace of mind.

In the nine months I've lived in my tony upper west side apartment, I have never seen an insect in the building; I had almost begun to believe that domestic vermin were a thing of the past, like chamber pots and dial-up internet. My roach-infested childhood seemed centuries ago. To be woken by the mother of them all goose-stepping up my thigh was rude indeed, a cruel joke by fate on the most neurotic of victims.

I scrambled out of bed and out of the room. I had a friend staying in the living room and so could not seek comfort in the untainted fold-out there. The bathtub was too short and the kitchen table too cluttered. In the tiny one-bedroom apartment, there was nowhere for me to hide. I had to return to my room and face the beast. I pushed the door open and flicked the light on and waited. While positioned outside the room and peering in as the door slowly swung shut, I heard a ruffle and saw what I could have sworn was, were I not prepped to expect the worst, a butterfly, fluttering across the room to where my pants hang on hooks. The door closed, leaving me in a panicked dialogue with myself, "Wait,.... no, wait,..--I didn't just see… what I think I saw,--did I??"

The uncertainty was too terrible and I forced myself to kick the door open once more, and as I did, again the flapping of wings, only now the brown butterfly wheeled around and brushed against my forehead before it careened off towards my wall closet, landed, smoothed its wings, and bore back on its haunches, primed for battle.

Needless to say I "lost my shit." A din of retching and lamentations replaced the early morning quiet of my abode, as well as senseless pleas to my bewildered guest to "shoot it"—we rushed out in our pajamas to Gristedes for roach spray but when we returned we found that we didn't know where to aim it. The roach was gone. Or, I should say, it was still there, probably hiding inside the closet, nestling in my delicates, dropping a super-sized birth-sack in every bra-cup.

Now my guest had to go to work and I was left alone with the monster. So I called the super. He served mainly to remind me of the hopeless futility of man, chuckling at my tears when I informed him of my unwanted visitor, and scratching his head and blinking when he opened my closet and found no mutant insect waiting in plain sight for a good clobbering. After a few timid sprays of Raid in the corners, and having picked up two jacket sleeves, only to find not a single mutant under either of them, he shrugged his shoulders, handed me the spray can, and shuffled away.

I was left with a mounting horror at the realization that there was nothing anyone could do about this outrage. Momentarily I considered moving back to San Francisco (leaving all of my stuff behind to prevent stowaways), but I realized that even for me that was unrealistic. I had to either find the roach and kill it or just wait for it to eat through all my skivvies, hoping it would eventually choke on some bit of synthetic lace and die. I decided to attempt an assassination, rather than risk its returning to my lap the next steamy night.

I picked out a hiking boot, but then remembered a bit of wisdom I had gained as a child battling the legions: Sneakers and hiking boots are no good for roach-stomping, as their soles are ridged, and when one strikes at the insect with them, it often happens that part of the insect, or even its entire organism, falls in between the ridges and remains unhurt. The roach panics and flees under the nearest piece of immovable furniture, usually a refrigerator or oak dresser, and, of course, you also panic, and start slamming the boot against the floor or glass tabletop or wherever you found the roach, and inevitably, wreckage ensues. Sometimes you catch part of the insect under the boot, such as a leg or wing, and have to keep from dry-heaving when you see the rest of it, flayed and dismembered, stagger off to die in a potted plant.

No, one needs a flat-soled shoe, perhaps a man's dress shoe or the standard flip-flop for the job. I chose one of my hostess's mules and approached my poor room again, which now stank with the unpleasantly sweet odor of roach poison, like someone really sweaty stuck a sugar cube between his buttcheeks and farted through it. Suddenly a disgusting thought gave me pause—the roach was some five times as large as the average house roach. To murder it would leave behind carnage too vast and gory to simply mop up afterwards (if I owned a mop), and would surely ruin any garment against which I might kill it. I had to find another way.

July 6, 2005: I have been sleeping in the living room for the past three nights. I only visit my old room to select necessary garments (usually the ones nearest the top of my drawers) and shake them out before dressing. When I come home at night I undress in the living room, crack my bedroom door, throw the worn garments in the general direction of my laundry basket, and slam the door shut again. I dread running out of clean clothes to wear, as that will necessitate spending several minutes in the bedroom sorting through the dirty laundry.

This terrifies me because I don't eat in my room, and so there's nothing much to keep vermin occupied with but in feasting on the residual body matter infused in worn socks, blouses, underwear. If the roach is anywhere, it's drunkenly stumbling through the pile of my soiled clothes, addicting itself to my pheromones, developing an ever-keener nose for my scent. Surely the moment I step into the room I'll look down and find that cockroach humping my big toe.

July 8th: Yesterday, in a moment of incomprehensible forgetfulness, I breezed right into my bedroom with nary a thought as to the danger that lay in wait for me there. In my obliviousness, I turned to my wall mirror and picked my mascara out of the tin cup on the shelf beneath it. Just as I was lifting the wand to my lashes, I caught sight of something else in the mirror, to the bottom right of my face.

I spun around. There, in full view, smugly eyeing me from atop my night stand, was the cockroach. It made no attempt to scurry away, hide, or even take flight; it just sat there like a sphinx, unmoving except for its antennae, inches long and all a-twirl. I half expected to see a lonely tumbleweed drift past us and hear plaintive whistling in the distance.

I reached down with my left hand, picked the plastic bag from Gristedes up off the floor, and slowly walked to the shelf. With wrath swift and god-like I swung the bag forward over the stand while with my mascara wand I knocked the beast into it, immediately tying the handles together in triple knots.

Crunch, crunch,.....crunchcrunchcrunch it went, imprisoned and frustrated. This Gristedes bag was the kind made of unusually thick, crinkly plastic, so every step the leviathan took crackled like hellfire, which I interpret as heavily symbolic.

I was about to take the bag outside and throw it into a waste bin when I realized that, as I was now safe, my molester all imprisoned, I could just leave it where it was and let it think on what it had done for a while. I turned the night stand lamp on next to it, so it might contemplate its sins in the harsh glare of righteousness. I slept that night in the living room.

July 10th, 2005: Crunch, crunch, crunch.... The prisoner, whom I now call Gregor, shows no signs of wilting. Three days with no food or water has had little discernible effect on his vitality. I examine his bag every few hours and watch the almost beautiful play of light and shadow he makes as he crawls this way and that, his body silhouetted against the wrinkled plastic walls, now sharper as he bears down close to the wall, now blurrier as he ruffles his wings and stretches his insect legs.

The scene is Chekhovian in its sadness: the seagull has wandered far from his home and rightful place and thus must die, unnaturally, and in a strange land. Crunch, crunch, crunch...I wonder how it all will end. I remember my mother telling me as a child that a cockroach can live for three months on a crumb of food too small for the human eye to see.

Perhaps Gregor will enjoy such longevity, crunching away on my night stand as summer ripens and fades into fall and the leaves start to change, as people marry and divorce, grandparents die and babies are born. He will wander till he expires in his crinkly white limbo, with only the memory of the bustling outer world, its sewers and basements, dropped ice cream cones and spilt soda, sleeping females and closets filled with silks, to sustain him in his final hours. Flights of angels sing thee to thy rest, my Gregor.

Note to self: Must buy new mascara.

Readers Response

Odious said, "The only way to get rid of cockroaches is to throw apples at them."

Sakaleen said, "Great information on your site folks. I also am working on a cat eye bead site. I'll bookmark yours if you bookmark mine. You can find it at cat eye bead. Again, nice site folks...I'll be baak..."

Omar said, "When I lived in West Africa I had some cats that ate my house roaches. Crunch crunch crunch in the middle of the night, usually from the environs of the toilet (it was the edge of the Sahara, and the local roaches drank there). I learned to smile at the sound. Tried hard to train American cats to do this, but never have had any success. Too much meow mix?"

Matthew R. Mullenix said, "That was the best cockroach exposition/memoir/essay I've ever read, hands down. Bravo! Let me say also that what you could really use there is a pet screech owl. There are some complications, like the Migratory Bird Treaty Act, but these can be overcome...

"Listen: When I was a teen in Panama I kept a small flock of screech owls in the basement. I don't mean any disrepect to New York, but Panamanian roaches are truly impressive; consider they shared our basement walls with a species of moth the size of a diner plate, I kid you not. Anyway, my owls killed and ate these roaches with extreme prejudice. Silent, feathered ninjas. I managed to sneek one or two of the birds into my bedroom at night and would (as Omar mentions above) enjoy the satisfying crinkle of beak on chitin that can only mean the owls were scoring big."

cube said, "Cockroaches are odious (no offense to odious intended) vile creatures and are not easily eradicated. Gregor will live a surprisingly long time in the bag. He might even begin to grow on you after a while...or maybe not."

Lee Kelley
Wordsmith at War

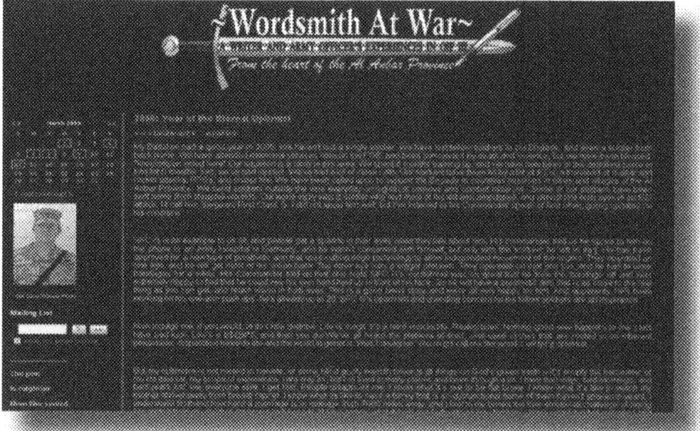

Lee Kelley is a freelance writer, blogger, and an aspiring novelist who has a passion for writing in all its forms. He is also an Army National Guard Officer who served for a year in Operation Iraqi Freedom during 2005-2006. He was stationed near Ramadi, Iraq, which is the southwest point of the infamous Sunni Triangle. After his deployment, he returned to Salt Lake City, Utah, where he works as an Emergency Communications Officer, is making up for lost time with his two children, and continues to write whenever he can.

Just Drop Me Off When This is Over

When this thing is over ...

Just drop me off on any Arizona or Utah highway, where the Buttes and the red rock canyons create optical illusions in the distance and across the horizon – I'll walk home.

Place me right at the top of a hill; I'll let gravity help me down.

Leave me on a back road in rural America, it doesn't matter where, so long as the leaves crunch under my feet and it is dusk and as I walk the shadows deepen and every so often I can see the lights from someone's house, and smell their cooking, and see families together on their couches watching movies, and hear their laughter.

Airlift me directly into a canoe in the middle of Black Creek in Missoula, Montana. It's fine, just leave me right there. I'll wet a hook for a while, then paddle to shore at dusk, enjoying the sound of the oars splashing in the clear, cold water. I'll clean the fish right there on the bank and cook it fresh over a small fire. Then I'll find the nearest road and hitch-hike home.

Believe me, it's no inconvenience.

Instead of transporting me directly to my home of record, according to my official military personnel file, do something spontaneous for me. When I get back to the States, blindfold me, and then leave me in a Pearl White Corvette Stingray or a rebuilt 77' Jeep Cherokee that has a 3 inch lift, with a full tank of gas, a sleeping bag in the backseat, a compass, and a map. Don't tell me where I am. Just leave me with my release papers and pat me on the back for my service to God and country. I'll remove the blindfold, crank the engine, turn on the radio, and start driving.

It doesn't matter what state or what city you leave me in - pick one. I'll have a grand adventure getting home.

Better yet, ask me where I'd like to be dropped off. I'll hop out right in front of my daughter's school. Its only 9 a.m. you say? That's just fine. I'll sit here on this nice wooden bench under this tree for a while. Leave me that newspaper, will you? Thanks. A little later I'll stroll up the street where all the fast food places are. I'll get a large fry at McDonalds and I'll put lots of salt on them. Then I'll get a Frosty at Wendy's. And I'll put all that with a Whopper with cheese, extra onion from Burger King. Perhaps I'll browse the shelves of the local Barnes and Noble after lunch and finish up with a cup of Starbucks Irish Cream coffee. By the time I get back to the school, it will be just about time for the bell, and I'll surprise my little girl and hold her tiny hand all the way home.

My son's daycare would be a fine place to drop me off too. I'll go in and check him out early. It may take him a minute to realize that Daddy's back, because he's only three, but I know he'll be very excited to see me. Then I'll take him with me to lunch and the bookstore, and to his sister's school. I'll walk all the way there with him on my shoulders. I'll buy him a Happy Meal with a toy.

Just get me on American soil.

Get me to New Orleans, and then put me in a taxi. I'll have the driver tune to a classic rock station that plays a lot of Queen and Styx and The Eagles and Steve Miller, or a nice Jazz station, and bring me straight to my parent's house to surprise them.

They'll be very pleased. I'll bring mom a dozen roses and dad the American Flag I flew for him in Iraq.

I don't sit around all day dreaming of home. We are too busy, and there is a lot of important work to get done.

It's when I sit down to write, and I'm trying not to bore readers with the little everyday mundane things that I do, that I get really nostalgic like this. I can't help it.

I honestly live an inspired life, and I am perfectly content to be here fighting in a war in

Iraq if this is God's plan for me right now, but that's because I know this too is transitory. I wouldn't want to stay here. It's not my home.

It is not America.

My children are young enough that they won't realize I was gone for so long until they're older. One day when they are teenagers it will dawn on them, and we'll be sitting around after a barbecue or something like that and I'll get a far away look in my eyes and realize that they're growing up too fast and that I am having an adult conversation with my children who were just starting Kindergarten when I went to Iraq.

And they'll say, "Wow, dad. You were really gone for a year and a half? I don't remember it being so long."

In fact, they're young enough that one more day won't matter. I know, I know, their mother will probably pull her hair out if I wait any longer than I have to.

But still, I mean it.

Open a road map of the United States of America, pick a cozy little town like Kinston, North Carolina or Gig Harbor,

Washington or Lafayette, Louisiana or Moab, Utah and just leave me there. It can be rock, asphalt, water, or sand -a busy college campus in New York or an abandoned park in Savannah, Georgia -the noise of a large highly populated metropolis, or the silence of the Appalachian Trail. Put me next to an interstate or next to a campfire - in a library or at a rock concert - in California or Maine.

Leave me in a nameless park, on a darkened street, or in a snowy canyon.

Don't ask me why. I don't want to explain it, and I can't explain it. But it will be fun and completely unplanned and I like the idea of that very much.

I'll have time to be utterly alone and think about a few things as I journey the last leg home to the life I left behind.

And I'll have a lot to think about.

So just drop me off, and let me drive out of the past, through the present, and into the unimaginable future of this crazy life.

"Not all those who wander are lost." *J.R.R. Tolkien*

Readers Response

Danielle Watson said, "You write very well, and I really enjoy reading your thoughts. Just one little thing: The quote is actually, "Not all who wander are lost." No biggie; I can just be a perfectionist about some things. Ask my husband if you see him, he'll roll his eyes and agree! (He is in SVC, Spc. Watson.) Keep up the good work. And thank you for your service."

Valerie said, "LT Kelley! You have gotta quit making me cry! It is amazing how so many who are here really take what we have for granted. Our scenery, our freedoms, our french fries! If nothing else good comes from this war (which something else good surely will! I am like you, an optimist!) there will be many who look at life a bit differently because of it. I know that I personally look at everything differently. I appreciate it all more. I appreciate my husband more.

"Thank you again for your talented way with words. Stay safe! And I know it is an odd request, but give my hubby a hug, wouldja? He needs one and I bet you could use one, too, so it would take care of ya both. Tell him it is from me!"

diane said, "I am right along with you on this. I was there eating those fries, and drinking that frosty. We really do take things for granted. You are such a talented writer, and really bring my emotions to the front when I read these blogs. Thank you and keep up the wonderful writing. You are an inspiration to many."

Subsunk said, "So few of us ever stop to really look at what we spent a good portion of our lives protecting. You, on the other hand, can't even look at it right now, but you've captured everything we like about America -- and

Americans. Put me down anywhere in the 50 states, and I'll find something to do, and find people I can love. You are wise far beyond your years, youngster. Press on."

We Support You

When you're in Iraq, mail becomes paramount.

No longer do you grab the stuff in your mailbox with the monotony that consumes after years and years of junk mail and coupons you'll never use. The walk to the mailbox is not a mechanical part of your day anymore. No more is your mail a constant trickle of companies reminding you that you owe them money.

Mail becomes a miniature Christmas, a small token or package or gift from a magical land far away that now seems kind of fuzzy in your memory like Santa and his reindeer through the glass of a child's globe which has just been shaken and presents you with a snowy winter-scape. A quickening of the spirit occurs when you receive a letter or package from your friends and family back in the United States. It must feel like a man receiving a message in a bottle after being shipwrecked on an island for years. This simile may be a stretch, but you get my drift.

Whether you are a true patriot, and you bleed red, white, and blue, or you are simply here because duty came knocking at your door, and you have some honor and some pride in what you do, it feels really good to receive thoughts and prayers from all of you back home.

You may be cooking one of us some home-made brownies this morning in a snug little town in the Blue Ridge Mountains of North Carolina, as you sip your Colombian coffee and enjoy watching the fog rise up off the slopes through your window, thinking about your son or daughter who is deployed in the Middle East.

You may send a photo of yourself snowboarding at The Canyons in Park City, Utah, and write "I missed you on the lift tonight," or some other inside joke in black marker right across the mountainous scene in the background to your friend in Iraq.

You may be retired. You may be a veteran, or a veteran of a foreign war. You may have been sitting in your living room just today writing a letter of appreciation on your favorite stationary and licking the seal and sending it to one of your grandchildren over here.

You may be a guy in Detroit who recently sent one of my Sergeants some new boots and a carton of smokes. He signed up on www.operationac.com to "sponsor" a soldier deployed overseas.

You may be a child, writing a letter in first period to a soldier from your hometown. We love the flags that you draw us in crayon or magic marker, coloring so carefully inside the lines. And we enjoy the intelligent letters you send us, wondering what it is like over here and if we are scared.

Whoever you are, and regardless of your political interests, or your feelings about the military or war or violence or our Commander in Chief, or Iraq, or Muslims, or the current stock market trends, we appreciate your support. Regardless of your favorite color, your skin color, the type of car you drive, your age, the college you went to, your lack of education, or your bad attitude towards teenagers and video games, we still thank you.

Because we are you. We are the American people, temporarily displaced for a spell in the Middle East. We exemplify virtually every race, class, profession, and opinion that you do over there across the pond. We're just fighting right now, that's all. We've been pulled away from "normal" life to serve our country as millions have done for America in past conflicts. Some of us believe in the political machines that nudge entire nations into war, and some of us just believe in ourselves and each other and doing the duty we raised our hand and swore to do.

Few know what fate waited for us behind that oath, but it took a special kind of person to make it either way.

We love our country with its high desert and thick forests, and coffee shops and bars and churches and fairs and malls and movie theaters and racetracks and bookstores and libraries and universities and quiet suburbia - a cul-de-sac street-lamp paradise, and football and Lollapalooza and children going down slides at countless parks and tattoo parlors and motorbikes and radio stations and cell phones and Thanksgiving and days off and fast food and sensible salads and backwoods and small towns and big city lights and Montana and Utah and New Orleans and Pennsylvania and the mid-west and the southwest and the pacific coast and the Great Lakes and A Prairie home Companion and Seattle and Texas and New York and watching our children take their first step, or hearing them say their first word, and shopping at Wal-Mart and Best Buy and Barnes and Noble and Starbucks Coffee and driving down winding roads, and our car stereos, and Barbecues and beer and our comfortable beds and the hugs of those we love and the spontaneous smiles of those we miss and believe me I could go on and on.

We listen to a lot of music over here and that music becomes the soundtrack of our lives. Country music, religious music, soft rock, heavy metal, rap, classic rock - we listen to it all, and it inspires.

You see – we don't ever forget. In fact, all we do is work over here, and remember. So please, don't let the media fool you. We are not the targets of the insurgency. YOU ARE. When the mass media shows you all the bad things that happen over here, the insurgents cheer. For they know they can never beat us. That's why they fight us the way they do. They are scared as hell, and they should be. This insurgency can never, ever defeat the American military.

But they can beat our hearts, they can cut of our inspiration, and they can do it through your TVs and your newspapers and your internet. For they know how embedded the media is in our society. They know that if we lose the support of the American public, we lose faith in ourselves. If the mass media had the inclination or the ability to show you all the good work we are doing over here, they would have 24 hour continuous coverage, 365 days a year, not American death toll statistics and instances of violence shown between recent Hollywood divorces and the latest headlines.

To a news channel, what makes better news, suicide bombers or the re-opening of a school in a small village that you will never even think about visiting? And what does the mass media really strive for, compassion or ratings? You decide.

If we, the Soldiers and Marines and Airman and Sailors and men and women of the United States Armed Forces lose your support, then the work we do will truly be in vain. Our inspiration will be dried up, our energy usurped.

If you are too proud to act patriotic and you feel like a hypocrite, then fake it. Do it anyway. Do it for us. Because like I said before, we are you. When you see us on TV, you're looking in the mirror. We are your sons and daughters and moms and dads and friends and neighbors. None of us could have known we would be in an ancient Holy Land in the year 2005, fighting a type of war that has never come before.

So don't cry for us, America, just pray for us. Don't worry, we know how to fight and protect ourselves. Just keep the light on for us, keep the house warm in the winter, wrap the pipes, offer us your support, look after our children, keep yourselves safe as you can until we return, and know that we stare up at the sky often and recall what it's like to be home.

Don't question our reasons for raising a hand a saying, "I do solemnly swear..." Just give us the benefit of the doubt. We're doing the best we can, and knowing you're behind us means a lot.

So Thank You, American people, for your continued support. Keep the care packages coming, and the brownies cooking. Send those letters. Take those pictures. Have the kids at school make banners. And if you're someone who doesn't know a soldier first hand, sponsor one. Take care of yourselves because it's a dangerous world. We worry about you.

We'll be back very soon to savor the American lifestyle once again.

And remember – no matter what happens, or where they send us -

WE WILL ALWAYS SUPPORT YOU.

Readers Response

melsisa said, "This actually brought tears to my eyes. I am printing a copy, I hope you do not mind, and I am submitting it to the paper. This is intense and heartening and real, and just some real good writing. We are so proud of you, and when you put things like that, the appreciation that I have for all of you is immense. Very powerful, and I know that you are speaking for yourself, as well as many others tht are there. Thank you for what you are doing, and remain strong, and keep writing. Thank you all, and god bless you as well as the people that live where you are."

Dan Fowler said, "Lt. This is your best yet and I read them all. Sure gave me something to think about. Maybe I can create a new compartment in my mind to accomodate all of my thoughts and feelings about a situation that upsets me greatly. Love.............Humptiesdump"

Randall said, "Dear LT. K, Working Army MARS related business with you was always a pleasure and reading your blog has given me additional insight to your character, intelligence and how lucky we are to have you in uniform. Looking forward to safe return, until then, know that I think of you often."

Major Chris Lachance, USAF

Desert Odyssey

I was deployed in support of Operations Enduring and Iraqi Freedom from 9 Sep 05 to 11 Jan 06. Before I left I created a blog primarily to keep in touch with family, but it became a place for me to practice writing and to vent frustrations/observations of what was going on in the world, and to show my views of life and family. Once I got home, due to the response I received from my website, I decided to keep it going. I have 2 kids and a third on the way, and am stationed in Tucson, Arizona currently. I have not published anything else besides my blog and the photo blog that I started recently.

My Views on the War

Ok...before I begin I need to reiterate that this is strictly my opinion (like everything else on here) and my opinion only. I'll surely hear from someone higher ranking than me about this one.

I've been watching what news I can about what is going on back home. In particular the political battles that have been waged over the past few months over how long we'll be here, how many troops have died, what the original reasons were for us getting into the fight, etc. I've mentioned a few times on here what my overall feeling is about the American politics and how it seems to have been working for a long time, but I won't go into depth on that here. What I do want to offer is my view as to why we're here, when we need to go home, and how much the political wrangling has helped us over here.

I have honestly no idea what happened with the Intel issues or whatever it is that the media and politicians seem so hell-bent on focusing on before we got over here. I don't know, or care, if Iraq had WMD in theater before we showed up. What I do know is that Saddam Hussein was a very bad man. He did very bad, unimaginable things to people. To women and children.

To celebrate he would go out on his porch and fire his rifle in the air in a display of his power. To this day, he is still an arrogant, delusional, psychotic killer. That was enough for me to go to war over here. What a lot of people seem to forget is that after the first Gulf War, we never left. My buddies and I have been deploying over here, flying over here, and getting missiles shot at us over here for 15 years.

With really no end in sight. So to hear that we had finally had enough and were going to go finish what we should have 15 years ago was a relief to me. WMD? Added bonus in my eyes.

The media hasn't really gotten on board with the whole Global War on Terrorism issue. What they seem to not understand is that this isn't an "Iraq War." It is a front in a global war. People think that if we just up and go that we'll be happy and safe at home and the reality is that that's probably not true.

These psycho's are everywhere in the world. And we are going to have to find them and get them everywhere in the world. If the bullets stopped flying in Iraq today my guess is that we'd be off to somewhere else real soon, to fight the same war, against the same enemy, on a different front. During World War II there were many fronts, but you didn't see politicians protesting the war in Japan, or women chaining themselves to the White House's fence because they're son died on Iwo Jima.

They understood that we were fighting a battle that needed to be fought, and because we were the only ones that could do it. It wasn't about American pride or arrogance or money, it was much simpler than that. Bad people in charge equals a bad world. I am not bragging about the US Military (as I will occasionally do)—I am merely stating a fact that we have the largest, most hi-tech, sophisticated fighting force on the planet. And as such, it is our moral obligation to fight the bad guys in this war. That's, in my opinion, why we came here in the first place and why we'll go on to the next front when it pops up.

Timeline for us to leave? That's an easy one. I'll start by disclaiming that again, I'm sitting in a cold CAOC hundreds of miles away from the marines (man they are so badass) fighting up range. I am, however, thousands of miles from a family that I love very much and miss with all of my heart. Every soldier up there has his opinion, and I would imagine that a few of them would really like to go home today. But I really think the vast majority of them, including the ones that have fought and died in this war (global war—not just Iraq) so far, would say the same thing I would to the president if I had the chance:

"Mr. Bush, I miss my home and my family. Bring us home when the job is done, and not one second sooner."

Ok. The political wrangling. I saw somewhere that people believe in Washington that slamming the doors of congress for a closed session, or holding an emergency "should we come home today?" vote portrays to the American soldiers over here the undying support and loyalty of congress. What it actually makes me want to say is "grow up." You want to support us? C'mon out here and say hi on Christmas Day when it will be just like every other day for us instead of staying with your family.

Donate as much money as you can to the thousands of young guys up there that volunteered to be here even though they barely make enough money to feed their wife and baby waiting back home. I am so tired of seeing CNN, Fox, MSNBC, broadcasting whines and complaints about how much they know what is right for us. Think about it guys. How much do you think a guy wearing combat fatigues, a 60-pound rucksack, covered with mud and carrying a rifle gives a sh*t (sorry) about a bunch of people bickering and complaining in suits and ties?

What cracks me up is that, like always, their opinions are conveniently split exactly down party lines. What a coincidence. You want to support us? Stop fighting. Unify like we claimed to have done after 9/11. I was never prouder of my government than when I saw all of them unite behind the president after the terrorist attacks. Where is that unity now? Drop the whole party line issue and vote/speak your conscience. Watching this on TV from over here is heartbreaking because it doesn't portray support, it portrays a divided group back home that can't decide if what we're fighting for is worth it.

Sorry for the ramble—didn't mean it to go on this far. I'll cheer it up a bit for tomorrow.

Readers Response

AirborneVet said, "Amen."

Anonymous said, "Rant - wouldn't it be so nice if each member of both parties could be cornered and forced to face up to what you said! As "the Bard" said "A pox on both your houses"."

Marcguyver said, "Lucky, you are so right on man! From this former Marine, Semper Fi! You can rest assured that there are still plenty of us Americans here at home supporting the heck out of you guys over there. Blessings to you and your family this Holiday Season and I hope that you get to see them soon, even if it is just for a short period of time.

"If you get bored, check out my sight: www.doneydepot.blogspot.com I'd love to hear from ya, it'd be an honor! Hang in there, keep your powder dry and your head down, and keep up the air supperiority for the boys on the ground!!"

Final Flight

I was golfing with a friend shortly after my return to Tucson, Arizona. One of the holes here runs alongside the Aircraft Maintainence and Recovery Center (AMARC), also known as "The Boneyard." Thousands of aircraft, when retired, are parked here in the sun in case parts, or the aircraft themselves, are ever needed again. The last duty I had prior to taking a break from my flying career was to shuttle my favorite aircraft, the T-37B Tweet, from Laughlin AFB in Texas to Davis-Monthan AFB, where the boneyard is. In a sick twist of fate, it was coincidentally also the base the Air Force was sending me to next.

While golfing down this hole, we noticed that the first line of aircraft behind the fence were the ones that I had personally flew in. My friend inquired as to whether or not I missed that part of my career. Words could not describe how much.

Readers Response

Trouble in Shangri La said, "Awww...you sound like a good friend of mine, a captain in the PD, who almost didn't take the captain's spot because he'd have to stop riding his bike (he was the Lt. over the motor squad so they let him keep riding as an LT)...I think he's still sad about it."

Richmond said, "I always thought that the boneyard looked like such a sad place... Apparently I was right. Great post, Lucky."

Stesphen P said, "Wonderful story. It makes me reminisce of our first loves. Thanks for sharing it."

Rude1 said, "I know just what you went (are going) through. I had the honor to place my F-5E into the "boneyard" years ago. I was a Crew Chief for 23 years, and the bond the pilots and CCs form with thier jets is hard to explain. You did a fine job; thanks for the memories."

Cowboy Blob said, "I used to pass that plane every day on the way to work (the AIA SCIF way down the flightline). Thanks for the story!"

El Capitan said, "I trained as an Air Traffic Controller out at Laughlin AFB back in 2000 before heading up to Alaska, and I loved talking the tweets down out of the pattern. Great planes to watch, and even better to fly. Every so often we'd get a flight with the excuse that we were monitoring the controllers.

"Ironically I ended up at Wright-Patt on the JPATS team. I got to help build and deploy the T-6A, soon to be T-6B. Great plane, and a blast to fly, but it'll never have the history the tweet did. Thanks for the story. It's nice to know that they all went out in style."

Melly
All Kinds of Writing

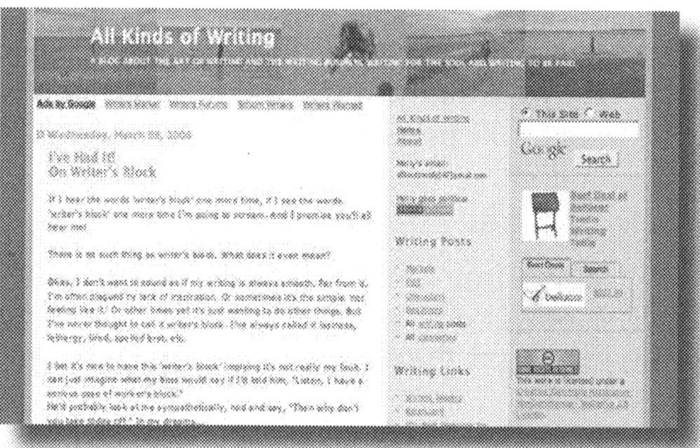

Melly writes fiction and articles for magazines and has been published both in electronic and print media. She lives in Toronto, Canada and started blogging in May 2005.

Writing and Cooking–It's All About the Feedback

I love cooking. Always did.

Yesterday I had guests over for dinner and so I spent the day cooking. (It was actually more like two hours, but who's counting?) I made split pea and ham soup, trout in dill and lemon sauce, and garlic mashed. Not a big deal meal, but still very nice I thought.

We sat to eat and immediately I could see that the soup was a hit. The bowls emptied out fast. Then we had the trout and mashed, and that's when the bread became very popular. I tasted the trout and to my horror, it was gross. I don't know what went wrong, but something did.

What does that have to do with writing?

In cooking, just like in writing, there is the issue of feedback and criticism. In cooking, just like in writing, the 'audience' has different personal tastes. In cooking, just like in writing, there is the question of target market.

Working backwards then, a meal cooked for kids would be different from one prepared for adults, just like when writing. As far as personal taste goes, the same dish could be a favourite of one person, but a nightmare to another, just like in writing.

And finally, different guests at a dinner party may have different ways of giving the cook feedback. One might try to drown the taste of the trout with bread, another would say very politely, 'I think there's something missing in the trout, but I'm not sure what,' and yet another, usually kids, would simply state the obvious, 'yuck!'

As a cook, I tend to prefer the direct 'yuck' approach. At least then I am able to offer something else and salvage that person's meal. As a writer, I have the distinct impression I would like the direct approach much better than having to decipher the true meaning of a feedback given to me in a roundabout way. If you're wondering, here's the code as I know it:

- 'This part was a bit slow for me,' means the writing was boring.
- 'I'm not sure what exactly you meant here,' means the writing was vague.
- 'I thought some of the word choices and language was a bit awkward,' meaning this part was poorly written.
- And my all time favourite - 'I understand this is your first draft, so I'll only comment on...,' means the writing was raw and bad despite it being your fifth draft.

How do you prefer to get your feedback? Wrapped in a blanket to cushion it, or thrown directly at you stone hard?

Readers Response

Jennifer said, "Ahhh...I like baking better, but I can cook when the occassion calls for it! Tell me what doesn't work. Don't beat around the bush, don't code your comments in vague words, just tell me what you think--honestly. The whole reason I have people read/critique my work is so I can find where it does and does not work. Hell if I didn't want feedback then I wouldn't ask you to read it! Just my take."

Josh said, "To be cynical for a minute: those four polite responses could just as easily be from a person who didn't bother to give your writing the attention it merited. I know for a fact that when I get too heavy in blog posts, people will post a comment that ends up being, for all intents and purposes, a complete non sequitur.

"Yes, you might see a few commenters who--on their good days would be quite astute--post some two-fragment nonsense reply about how "Man! it's SOOOO hard to cook fish!" or, as my first thought was, quote one of my favorite scenes from the movie Strange Brew. "I'll have two bowls of split plea soup, please."

"The point of my ramble is this: you should always vet your critics, making sure that you are getting good feedback. In my mind, having someone tell you "Hrrm. That paragraph was a tad wordy" after you've seen them misspell "dog" a handful of times should be a check against your wannabe editor, and should not be allowed stand as the final say on the matter. I also think that abrasive critics, so often lauded in the culture today as "unafraid to speak their minds" are often just sour jackasses with an axe to grind.

"OR maybe I'm just bad at what I do, and need a well-crafted rationale for dispensing with all criticism."

Pat Kirby said, "I like my feedback honest, but diplomatic. If the writer is on the defensive, if the writer feels "attacked," then the writer isn't absorbing all the information presented. There are some good articles about diplomatic critiquing over at Critters.

"But audience is a factor. One of my "funniest" worthless critiques came with a short story (contemporary fantasy.) The person whinged about the contemporary setting saying that it threw her out of the "fictional dream" (snerk). She complained about my use of green chile and New Mexican foods and suggested I make up fantasy spicy foods.

(Even on rejection, the story has been well received, so I know the premise works.) Hello? Contemporary fantasy. That's the point. A CONTEMPORARY SETTING. Bummer about the trout; sounded good. I don't eat pork, so I would have been eating a lot of bread at that meal."

Carter said, "Honesty is the best policy, in my book. I've been through several different critique groups (yes, I have some self-confidence issues), and I have developed a very thick hide. Puncture it if you can. My feeling is: get to the point so we can both move on. I make my own decisions about the worthiness of the advice, and I realize that different people have different opinions. That doesn't make us enemies. If I ask for a crit, it's because I want the story to be the best it possibly can be, so have at it hammer and tongs."

Melly said, ""Hell, if I didn't want feedback then I wouldn't ask you to read it!" Exactly my feelings, Jennifer, so why sugar coat everything or sound vague? Beats me!"

Melly said, "Non sequitur - ouch Josh, you touched on a sore subject. I don't know if people don't pay attention or just being... well, you know what, but sometimes some of these comments, man... Not here, though. I love the comments I get here, usually way more profound than the post I wrote.

"So, you're saying, speak your mind, be honest, but not brutal? I agree with that too. No need to sugarcoat, but not to be needlessly ruthless? Doubt you suck at what you do, btw, judging from what you've been doing at the WBA."

Melly said, "Oh, yes, of course. Attacking's no good. Imagine if my guests attacked me yesterday, knives and all, wouldn't have ended well.

"You're so right, is depends a lot on who critiques you. I have this one friend, a writer too, that when this comes from him - listen Melly, this really isn't that good - I accept it for what it is because I know he appreciates my writing otherwise and I know that we think alike. So he can be as straight as they come with me.

"With others though, people who I don't know as well, or who think very differently from me (re that person who critiqued your contemporary fantasy story) I'd probably need to hear it more diplomatically.

"Hey, you and the J-man are always welcome for dinner. I promise I won't make any pork."

ME Strauss said, "Welcome back, Melly. Great post--nice analogy."

I like my feedback specific, especially if I can act upon it or discuss it. I like to know the reasoning behind the comments so that I can decide whether I need to do something or it would just *be nice.*

"When it becomes a discussion the reader sometimes sees where a quick surface change he or she is suggesting might unravel many things, but together you find a new solution that is better than the old and the first suggestion. That's ideal, I know (BIG GRIN) Oh yeah, and I like it to be fun."

Melly said, "I like that, Carter. I would like to think I have a thick hide, but in all honesty, I probably don't. And again, it depends who says it more than how they say it. Self-confidence is such a problematic issue when it comes to our writing, isn't it? It's like I'm two different people: one for daily life with normal self-confident, the other for my writing with almost nil self-confidence. Why is that???"

Melly said, "Thanks, Liz. I was busy... cooking...

"Absolutely, without reasoning the writer can't really figure out if a change is necessary, or what it is exactly that needs changing. But sometimes it's hard to give reasoning. Sometimes you just love or hate a piece. You can analyze it, but still the feeling is there, unexplained.

Ideal, fun, discussion, happy... I don't know... sounds so... nice... Are you sure we're talking about the same thing? Just kidding, of course."

Melly said, "Oh, and Pat, sorry, I forgot to thank you for the link. Will definitely look at it."

dog1net said, "Good analogy. I like the flavor of this post."

Melly said, "Hey there, dog1net. Well, as long as it's not the trout's..."

Cavan said, "When I'm getting feedback - bite, scratch, maim - tear whatever I've written to shreds. I need that to know what I'm doing wrong (and chances are I'm doing wrong more often than I'm doing right). That said, I also need to be praised, and I don't mean in a mindless "your story was sooooo good, I loved it, it's so totally like the best thing I've read... ever" kind of way). Basically, I need to be told what's great about my work and what sucks. Only then can I know what to keep and what not to. Generally, I can tell when a reviewer dislikes the story because they think its poorly written and when they dislike because it's just not their taste. In fact, on my blog I recently asked for beta readers for a short story I'd completed. One of those who responded told me that my story was decent, but instead of focusing on this character it should've focused on that character, and instead of being about this it should've been about that.

His points were rather interesting, but ultimately, he just wasn't interested in my story and wanted the concept I'd come up with to be used in an entirely different fashion."

Jean said, "I can't fix it if I don't know what's wrong or can't break your code. If I'm writing something for publication (yes, for some strange reason, that is my goal), I need to know if it isn't working. I don't have much experience with getting feedback, so I'm sure my hide isn't thick enough yet, but it needs to get thicker. Please help. So far, nobody has hurt my feelings. I can usually see exactly what someone means when they point out a problem and tend to agree.

"As Monica Jackson said, she can bring out the stiletto heels and tap-dance all over the manuscript or she can (while banging her head on the monitor) tell you everything's just fine. I think stiletto heels, thoughtfully applied, would result in a more marketable manuscript. Bring 'em on."

Melly said, "Wow, Cavan, 2 excellent points. Tell me the good stuff too and be just as brutally honest about that. Of course we need to know what we're doing well, not just what we're doing bad.

"Your other point - the distinction between someone not liking a story because it's poorly written or because it's not his/her taste makes a lot of sense. You'd take the criticism in a whole different light. In fact, I think this is perhaps what

Pat was saying too, but me being the thick person that I am took it the wrong way.

Melly said, "Love your analogy, Jean! Seems to be a consensus amongst us writers. I don't know, maybe we do develop a thick hide with all those rejection letters. Maybe we can accept criticism much better. Stiletto heals is."

Patry Francis said, "Very interesting subject, Melly and I love the cooking analogy.

"Unfortunately all criticism is not created equal. Discerning which criticism to accept and utilize and which to ignore is one of the most important skills a writer can develop. For that reason, I like my criticism honest, detailed and well-reasoned. No attack dogs or stiletto heels on my heart, but no Hallmark cards either."

Melly said, "Patry, you're so right. It's not just how to "accept" criticism but it's learning how to "discern" it. Okay, I'll keep my dogs leashed with you..."

Eric Mutta said, "As a programmer, I view the writer-reviewer relationship the same way as the programmer-hacker relationship.

"On the left side of said relationships, you have the creators. They have to synthesize ideas, actively searching the maze within all creative minds, then immortalise their conceptions in ink. On the right side, you have the destroyers. With very little effort, they can savagely shred a piece to bits in the time it takes one to blink. Before I started writing publicly, I spent an awful lot of time reading people's reviews of movies, books, etc. I came away with the following:

- 90% of reviews are next to useless for the advancement of the writer.

- If someone is writing a review, then congratulations: either you impressed them or you really ticked them off.
- The best reviews come from those who could have themselves written what is being reviewed.

"For my writing, I welcome all reviews, especially those from the raving savages who believe it is their duty to tear your work apart. You see, if you humbly point out the lack of anything resembling a neuron inside those craniums of theirs, they will retaliate by telling the whole world about it. In doing so, they achieve two things: making a mockery of themselves, and advertising your work to people who wouldn't otherwise have known about it...Call it writer's Judo."

"PS: what on earth are split peas? (Having found his first target, Eric goes off to start the RSPCV - Royal Society for the Prevention of Cruelty to Vegetables."

Dana said, "How do I prefer my feedback? Directly, but with some respect. I wouldn't want to hear, "Your story sucks raw eggs." I would prefer something like, "Dana, this needs a lot of work in (insert sections) if you want it to sell."

Sorry about the trout. Good post! And thanks for commenting on my blog today."

Lee Carlon said, "I've never had a problem telling people their food sucks, if it's no good I just can't eat it. Breaking the news to a writer on the other hand I'm not so good at, I try to find diplomatic ways to say things, having studied communication in one of my jobs I know that people react to, and understand, positives quicker than negatives. So instead of saying, 'your main character was poorly written and undeveloped,' I'd say 'you need to bring out more of your main character's personality and flesh him out,' not a huge difference between the two, but I think it would make a difference to the author, and as Pat said, there really is no point putting the author on the defensive because they'll miss most of what you're saying, and then you're wasting everybody's time."

Melly said, "Shame on me. I'm not sure about the difference between programmer and hacker, Eric, even if I think I was one (or the other) at some point. Now to the all important question - what are split peas? They're usually field peas that are dried and then split. When soaked (like in soup), they get soft again and yummy. So... you're going for the "negative publicity" stint? I admit I more often than not wanted to do the same, but alas, I'm a chicken shit. Good for you, take it like a man, and give it like a man!"

Melly said, "*"Your story sucks raw eggs."* - That's hilarious, Dana. Yeah... the trout.. oh well, what can you do? I'll be coming to see you often. I love discovering new blogs."

Melly said, "Lee, you're my kind 'a guy! When it comes to cooking feedback. You and Pat are smart people. I've seen writers go on the defensive and then they can't get anything else into their heads. It turns into an argument rather than a feedback session.

Shirazi said, "Fine points that I am going to take. Thanks."

Melly said, "Always good to see you here, Shirazi."

Erasmo Nault said, "I really appreciate people like you who take their chance in such an excellent way to give an impression on certain topics. Thanks for having me here."

Melly said, "Erasmo, sorry, seems I've missed your comment. Thank you!"

Dark Matter in Art, in Writing

It's been a while since we talked science, and don't you worry, we'll get to writing too. Today, I finally caught up on some of my science news of the past week. Seems that I missed a lot of news about Dark Matter. To those unfamiliar, a quick explanation from Wikipedia:

In cosmology, dark matter refers to hypothetical matter particles, of unknown composition, that do not emit or reflect enough electromagnetic radiation to be detected directly, but whose presence can be inferred from gravitational effects on visible matter such as stars and galaxies.

Just to explain it a little bit further, or more plainly perhaps (and those who know better are welcome to add and correct), it was argued back in 1933 by Zwicky that the gravity of cluster galaxies is insufficient to hold it together, and that there must therefore be additional gravity from dark matter, or otherwise the cluster would fly apart.

One news item I missed seems to have given the final proof:

> [...]an Israeli cosmologist showed that the existing model of elliptical galaxies was wrong, proving that dark matter was there all along.

(Of course that this still isn't a smoking gun, but it is sufficient to continue assuming in dark matter's existence).

Now let's switch gears. You may recall that two posts ago I questioned what is art. I claimed that art is beyond skill and beyond creativity. I claimed that art is something that combines all of these but I was hard pressed to find an exact definition. Then, in my comments, ObilonKenobi said that art is more than the sum of its parts.

Well, I think that's just it. What makes art art? What makes a good book art? Dark Matter.

That invisible, undetectable something that helps bind the sentences, the paragraphs, the ideas, the plot, the characters in a way that is more than simply the sum of its parts. Something we cannot necessarily pinpoint or see but that we can identify its existence when it is present. It helps bring a good book together and hold it there in what we call a work of art.

Maybe if scientists one day find a way to 'see' dark matter, that would also be the day in which we'll find a way to identify artistic dark matter.

Readers Response

Jennifer said, "Do you think we'd really be able to find that 'artistic dark matter'. I always thought that each persons talent their 'dark matter' was unique to each person. It worked its own way for each different person. Though maybe that's the inspiration that works differently for everyone. And the actual talent is some how defined...

"It's a tricky topic to discuss. I have a hard time putting thoughts into words and sentences that make sense and explain how I'm thinking. But I do like the terminology you've give this unexplainable: Artist Dark Matter!"

Melly said, "Why thank you Jennifer. I wasn't looking from the artist point of view, but rather from the spectator, reader point of view. I guess though you can also look at it from the artist's pov - identifying artistic dark matter for the artist's sake."

ObilonKenobi said, "As I am both a fan of art and science I appreciate the comparison of elusive Dark Matter in the universe to the "Dark Matter" that makes art special. There are some artists and artworks that just define a movement and even a generation. So many people have tried and failed to find that "It" factor, the "Dark Matter" that holds together all the elements that make something or someone a "Happening," a "Movement," or a "Defining Moment In a Generation.

"Believe me I have tried myself. I studied art and writing. I look for that combination of things that makes it happen. I don't think there is any scientific combination there is only a wispy elusive "thing." Unlike the Dark Matter that makes the gravity necessary to hold the universe together by just that much, the "Dark Matter" that makes art beautiful and inspiring will never be found or proved. That's why when I look at the universe and all the physics that define the laws of how things work I do believe that there is something more that we can never grasp or define."

Melly said, "That's why you're a Jedi master.ObilonKenobi - you're a believer. I still hope for that one theory that could explain it all. I know I will never know it even if it is out there (which I'm not sure it is, in which case we revert back to your 'something more'), but I can hope.

easywriter said, "An excellent post Melly. Dark Matter Art! This makes art seem as mysterious and elusive as... perfection.

Melly said, "Thanks Easywriter. I was due for one... I love how you put it."

easywriter said, "Melly, I have yet to read one of your posts that wasn't well thought out and wonderfully presented. You do very well!"

Melly said, "Oh, my. Blush."

Teh Blog Father said, "'What makes art art?'"

How about this definition: Everything sucks. That which is art, is art because it sucks less."

Melly said, "Ummmm, I like your aesthetics definition better."

dog1net (Scot) said, "Melly: Perfect post to ponder over on such a rainy night. Robert Pirsig (Zen and The Art of Motorcycle Maintenance) developed in an interesting argument in regard to how we recognize what we perceive as "art." As he says, "The sun of quality . . . does not revolve around subjects and objects of our existence. It does not just passively illuminate them. It is not subordinate to them in any way. It has 'created' them. They are subordinate to 'it'"

"Even still, much to think about.

Enjoyed . . .

Scot"

Melly said, "Whoa! I'll have to really think about that one. Very complicated concept.

Thanks, Scot."

Teh Blog Father said, "'Ummmm, I like your aesthetics definition better.' I figured you would (grin).

"PS: Teh Blog Father = Eric Mutta

"PPS: the sentiment behind that less appealing definition above, comes again from the software world. Because the field is so young (about 60 yrs. old), the state of the art su-, I mean, is still rather shoddy."

Melly said, "Eric, I know you're teh blog father. What'dya think??? I'm not certain I understood your last comment. Which field is young, software?"

redchurch said, "Rather than Dark Matter I tend to view it as Heisenberg's Uncertainty Principle. You can measure the state of an electron, it's spin or it's movement in time or space but not both at the same time. To me this like story structure vs. active writing (plotting vs. drafting) - You can actively plot your story out, but while you do this you're not actively writing. You're just making plot points. All the plotting in the world won't get your story done, you still just have to write. But if I merely get lost in the flow of writing, my story may not have the cohesion, clarity, and compelling structure it needs.

"So the two are at odds with one another, and you can't really do both simultaneously. At any given time you have to choose one or the other, or set a procedure or sequence that allows each to have their time and place.

"It's a difficult balance that I feel applies to most forms of creativity. You have the theoretical, principles, structure, planning, and then you have the actual activity of creation which in many ways defies organization and classification. I believe the two can be balanced, but I won't pretend finding the balance is easy."

Teh Blog Father said, "'Eric, I know you're teh blog father. What'dya think???' Just checking (innocent smile).

"*'I'm not certain I understand your last comment. Which field is young, software?'* Yes."

Terry said, "Since art is so subjective, and each viewer has his or her own definition of what constitutes art (i.e., paint daubs, graffiti or wrapping an island in plastic), are you saying that dark matter is also subjective, and may or may not actually exist depending on who "views" it?

"Or did I not get the whole thing? (it happens...)"

Melly said, "redchurch, I loved your analogy. So true."

"Eric, you should read *Snowcrash*. I think you'll like it. It's about the beauty in programming (among other things)."

"Terry, you assume I agree with you about the subjectivity of art. I don't really, and therefore don't think dark matter is subjective. I'm a bit of a snob when it comes to art... Sorry..."

Mark said, "I love how you were able to take two, apparently, conflicting arenas – science and art – and blend them into one through the concept of black matter. Nicely done. Actually it made black matter easier for me to grasp by doing that."

Terry said, "Hi, Melly. No worries. I'm a bit of an art snob myself these days. We'll agree to disagree on that then."

Melly said, "Mark, wow. I think that this is one of the nicest things anyone's ever told me. Terry - agreed."

ObilonKenobi said, "Melly, by the way. I have to say your postings are great. SO much to talk about. I'm not sure art is meant to be grasped by any one person or theory. I think it a personal experience. Great art is a personal experience shared by many in the same way but different. I am not sure that someone who looks at a Cubistic painting gets the same evocative feelings that I do. There's a whole slew of history there some my own personal experience with the art, some I've read about the artist, some of the time it was created and some just ethereal and unable to be pinned down.

"I happen to be a big fan of Cubism and Picasso in particular. It's just my personal feeling. Many people share my opinion of his greatness but I highly doubt they share it in the same way because the teachers who introduced the art to me were not the same as well as the people I went to the museums with to view it for the first time. Great art can encompass a whole history into one painting and become something more, as I said."

"Redchurch, "Rather than Dark Matter I tend to view it as Heisenberg's Uncertainty Principle. You can measure the state of an electron, it's spin or it's movement in time or space but not both at the same time." Of course I love physics so I do love the analogy. This is my kind of forum where physics and art mix freely. I also agree that outlining and writing are like quantum mechanics. Great way to put that concept into perspective."

"The Blog Father, yo'."

"As for Dark Matter, I think the analogy is that it's something that's out there. We know it's there but we can't see it, describe it or tell you what it is exactly. That's the same with art. What makes good art? We can't really tell you but we'll know it when it's there and when it's not there we know that too. Like Dark Matter we know it's there because of what it does to the universe. We just know it's there just like when we know art is good. I don't think the analogy goes as far as saying that Dark Matter is subjective.

"Of course to confuse you more, in Quantum Physics there is the theory that the observer makes the outcome by predicting what will happen. A state does not exist until someone observes it until then it exists in a sort of non-state, and in-between. Observation makes reality. In that way the universe doesn't exist unless we are here to observe it and the paradox is that we aren't here unless the universe exists... OK my head hurts."

Melly said, "So much great material for next posts... Thanks ObilonKenobi."

Meryl K. Evans
Meryl's Notes

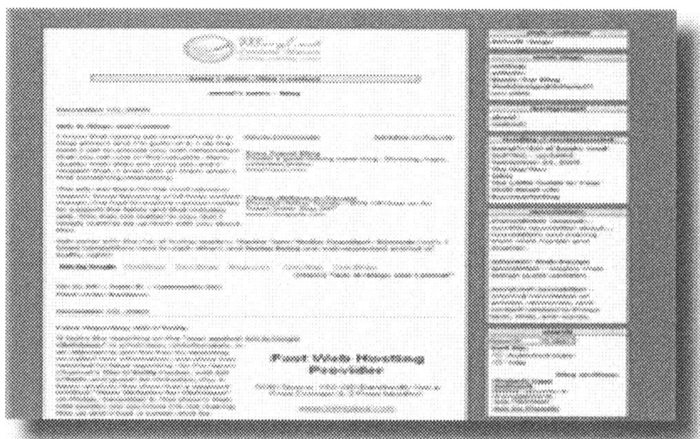

Meryl K. Evans is the Content Maven behind the *eNewsletter Journal* and *The Remediator Security Digest* newsletters. She is also a *PC Today* columnist and a blogger at *InformIT*. The native Texan has three children and a husband to keep her on her boots.

Other blogs:

Bionic Ear blog
InformIT Blog
Contributor to Stories of Strength:
Regular Web site

Apostrophe Spaces

Teresa Gomez writes, "I have a question for you concerning the use of apostrophes. I was an English major in college and I even managed to graduate with a BA in English. However, my son is being taught in his 5th grade class that he must allow a space when writing a word that includes an apostrophe.

"For example, he wrote can't and was marked down because his teacher requires a space separating the cursive letters where the apostrophe is inserted. Another mother and I discussed this and she agrees with the teacher. Did I miss something in my education requiring this space?"

This is the first I've heard of this practice. My daughter is in 5th grade and she writes apostrophes in the same way Theresa and I do—no space. I verified with my daughter and she said her school does it both ways—it doesn't matter.

I searched my reference books and the Internet. Didn't see anything pointing out this practice. The few resources I did find indicated there is no space, but the resources weren't major or well-known resources. Anyone heard anything? Obviously, adding the space is going to lengthen handwriting time and so few people still do handwriting beyond grade school as is.

Readers Response

Wizard Prang said, "I've never heard anything about this "space-with-apostrophe" practice. But then I'm a Brit - what would I know about the English Language?"

steven vore said, "Are they specifically talking about cursive writing, that the pen be lifted between the 'n' and the 't' of "can't" - if so, that almost makes sense, but seems real nit-picky to me. If, on the other hand, they're talking about print or type and want "can' t" or "can 't" then I think that's absolutley absurd."

Alan said, "I really hope that this is only about cursive writing. In cursive writing it is incorrect to join the "n" and "t" in can't, this would make the word *can't* with something peculiar between the "n" and "t." But this is not a space.

There cannot be a space between the "n" and "'," the apostrophe here marks missing letters prior to the "t." This would give the word can and another two-letter word ending in "t." A legitimate form of apostrophe, if somewhat rarely used, is in e'er for ever. Not e 'er, where the 'er is recognisable English for her. I do not want to e her see her again. Think not.

There are many uses of apostrophe, none require a space when it appears at the end or in the middle of a word. Obviously, if the apostrophe is at the beginning of a word a space is there to separate the words. Said with almost total confidence!"

meryl said, "Alan, yes, they're talking handwriting."

richard said, "Hmmm... when I write can't in cursive, the tail of the 'n' doesn't connect to the upstroke of the 't'. It's not a real space, just a small break between the letters. I'm pretty sure that's the way we were shown how to do it all those years ago, way back in the late 70s. Write the 'can' then the apostrophe, and then the final 't'..."

Louisa said, "I have taught English for 34 years. In cursive writing, there is to be a separation of letters/space when an apostrophe is required. I think it is wonderful that some teachers still demand perfection."

Chris Howard

the0phrastus

I've been blogging over a year now, and I'm just starting to put together some stats for my site. I just picked up the SaturdayMorningWritingClub.com domain name, and I'm trying to get my wife to run something like an informal workshop for young writers, or at least a destination site for ideas, materials, essays and links to writing information. I don't know if we'll get it off the ground.

My book site: **http://www.lykeionbooks.com/thewreath**
My Aristotle site: **http://www.non-contradiction.com**

Saturday Morning Writing Club

Or how a fourth-grade girl co-authored a novel that you can buy at Amazon.com.

Two years ago on a Saturday morning in December, my daughter Chloe started "Saturday Morning Writing Club." This wasn't really surprising at the time because she started new clubs every week. She already had a Harry Potter Club, Magic Club, Reading Club, and pulled her brother, Christopher, into all of them. I'm not sure if club forming is a common practice for fourth-graders or girls or kids in general. I know my brother and sister and I started a club once, but it centered on us. Our first names all started with C and there are three of us, so naturally, we formed the CCC club. I don't remember doing anything as part of this club, but I think there's something desirable from a kid's perspective of creating a structure, even an arbitrary one.

At the time, I was writing an historic novel about Aristotle, envisioning three or four books, one for each of the significant parts of his life. In the biographies about him, especially from a philosophical perspective, Aristotle's life is broken into three big segments, his early student days in Athens at Plato's Academy (and likely, Isocrates' school as well). The second part has him moving to what is now western Turkey, taking up residence and philosophizing under the sponsorship of Hermeias, ruler of Atarneos. Aristotle married Pythias, Hermeias' adopted daughter (probably a niece).

The second part ends with Aristotle moving back to Macedon, tutoring Alexander (who became The Great), before returning to Athens to form his own school, the Lyceum (Lykeion is the transliterated Greek). The final act of his life ends with him departing Athens in his early sixties, allegedly telling an angry mob he would go before they sinned against philosophy a second time. (The first being the death of Socrates). I added a fourth part, his childhood, growing up in Macedon, the son of the physician to the King of Macedon, the foundation period before he headed to Athens at 17.

So, there I was, two years ago, two-hundred thousand words into part one, and struggling against historic constraints, when Chloe started Saturday Morning Writing Club. Like most of Chloe's clubs, this one was loosely organized. There was a "sign-up sheet"--which I gladly signed--and a brief discussion of the rules and mission of the organization. Then we sat down, me with my computer and Chloe with her notebook, and started writing at the dining room table, also known as the Slytherin Common Room Table.

(We were renting a house off Ocean Blvd. in North Hampton at the time, and although it didn't come furnished, it came with a table. The owners probably didn't want to move the giant greenish-black marble slab--on a big pedestal block of the same stone--from the dining room. Salazar would have been pleased with its cold hard surface). The first Saturday it was just the two of us clacking at the keyboard and scratching on paper. The second Saturday, I started explaining the writing process to Chloe. You know how it goes when you teach something: you end up learning a lot yourself because you're forced to dig into the subject and really understand it in order to explain it to someone else.

I asked her to tell me what she wanted to read about if she could read anything. Mermaids. Okay, so I got some 11x17 paper and drew eight equal-sized boxes, numbering them 1-8. Who's your main character? A girl. It must be a girl, a strong girl. Chloe asked me for a name, so I picked Kassandra, a good Greek name with a lot of meaning behind it, and I had to spell it with a K (kappa), not the Latinized C.

Is Kassandra successful in the end? Yes. I wrote, "Kassandra succeeds" at the top of the eighth box.

We spent another couple Saturdays filling in the seven other boxes with major scenes, leaving the climax for later when we understood the story better. We also built Kassandra's world during this time, a city at the bottom of the sea. We asked ourselves a hundred questions: Where is it located, why is it there, who lives there, social structure, history, family lines, religion, economic structure. And there were a couple weird questions we surfaced, like what do they eat and how do they cook it with such high pressure and cold temperatures?

I had to explain to Chloe that you don't actually use the world-building exercise to stuff the story full of facts, and it's not even used to justify this city at the bottom of the Atlantic. Most of world-building work is used to give the writer the confidence to work comfortably in this new world, giving her the sense of reality that our world has if she was writing about a girl, for example, growing up in Massachusetts.

Up to this point I didn't think I was going to be the principle writer of this story. It was Chloe's story. I was just trying to explain what I do late at night during the week and every Saturday morning. She's a huge Harry Potter fan, although she reads just about anything, and has other favorites, Wilder's Little House series may even hold a higher place.

Chloe loves the magic of Harry, but one of her motivations for The Wreath of Poseidon (our working title) was that there aren't enough strong girls in YA genre fiction. I think there are. Some of the characters created by Garth Nix and Tamora Pierce come immediately to mind, but there are many. You just have to look around. Of course, her answer would be that there's always room for another strong female lead.

Story telling lessons: First, I had to tell Chloe that I'm a total amateur at this writing thing. I've been writing for years, and it seems like I spend all my waking hours writing, but not many people have seen my work, and even now, two years later, things have only moderately improved. Second, I had to make it clear to Chloe that no one wants to read about a girl without any problems, nothing to struggle against, happy, at peace, and with everything she wants. Boring.

I used Harry Potter, something that Chloe knows very well, to explain story structure. Kassandra's kind of a loner, without a lot of friends. Kassandra might be miserable, but she has to have some friends, even if their real purpose in the story is the betray, help, explain details about the world, etc.

Look at Ron Weasley. Harry's friend knows very little about the muggle world, but loads of stuff about the wizarding world. One of his purposes in Rowling's story is to explain things to Harry. The reader perceives this as necessary and well within probability. Harry's a newb, and here's this guy who knows it all. Of course he's going to tell

Harry. It just has to work naturally. No one will read the book if the narrator pops in every couple chapters with a forty page essay on how this new world works. This is the simplest way to destroy a story...unless you're Victor Hugo. Even Ron Weasley has a much larger role than explainer. He's a friend, a fellow Gryffindor, with a whole family of characters who are integral to the plot. So, the explaining itself has to fit into the world. It has to be real.

I told Chloe it's a mistake to have Kassandra "overhear the butler and maid" telling the reader about stuff every character in the story already knows. The reader will perceive this as an obvious contrivance. If you're going to have Professor Brain enter the story with a dissertation on the uses of compressed plasma trails in building a time machine, the old boy better be a real part of the story, not an obvious set piece that the author has shoved in to tell the reader something. (What's interesting is that if you go with a restrained approach, pushing in bits of backstory here and there, sometimes you end up with too much. There was a doctor who examines Kassandra, finding all kinds of odd things about her (ear infection, weird blood chemistry) in one version of chapter two, but we cut her out of the story completely because it slowed the plot down. I still think chapter 2 is too long, but that's what we went with).

We spent a lot of time discussing what causes story tension, what makes a story suspenseful. Some ideas were Chloe's, some were mine. I created the idea of a wreath as a device, a hereditary source of power, something that's passed from parent to child. Some were both of ours: You want misery? You can't go wrong with an orphan, an oppressive governess, a phobia, rivalries.

In short, I really got into this new story about Kassandra and the world we'd created. When Chloe asked if I would write it with her help, I dropped Aristotle, and became a full, participating member of Saturday Morning Writing Club. My only condition was that it become a story that I would also like to read, not just a kid's story, something with a little depth, some subtly, not a lot but enough to satisfy an adult reader. Chloe was fine with this, and that night at The Galley Hatch, a family restaurant in Hampton, New Hampshire,

I wrote the first line of The Wreath in Chloe's notebook. I know a writer shouldn't become attached to any particular line or paragraph, but I have resisted changing the first line throughout the work, and that's the line that went into the final: Gregor's fingers tightened around the cold ring of chrome. If I have a message in this post it's that writers with kids should try getting them into storytelling--and learn something in the process. It's not everyone's thing, so I wouldn't expect a lot of success. But you won't be disappointed with the ideas they generate. (If you have kids, I'm not telling you anything you don't already know. They're shockingly brilliant at times, right?).

My son, Christopher, just doesn't want to be a writer. He joined the Saturday Morning Writing Club at some point, but only with pressure from his older sister, and he never really participated. He does show up every now and then with some great lines of a dialogue, which I've used, and a couple cool plot ideas. One that comes to mind has to do with symmetry. He was studying symmetry in school at the time, but the unique way he explained it, gave me a great idea that eventually went into a story. We don't have Saturday Morning Writing Club every Saturday anymore, but it's established, and it's always there, ready to go when we are. It can be any time or place, when neither Chloe or I have anything to do, and one of us will ask, "Do you want to do Saturday Morning Writing Club?"

Write on...

Readers Response

Deborah said, "I loved the idea about the eight boxes, Chris. I've tried in the past to get my sons interested in writing and blogging, but with no success.

For Christmas, I got them some art sets, along with some instructions on how to make comic books. Perhaps I'll be successful through this medium."

Chris said, "I know it's not easy. With Chloe, she wanted to write, but whenever I try to get my son into writing, he's says no. He likes to read (non-fiction more than fiction), and he loves to draw, but for now, the closest he gets to storytelling is to go through my Latin dictionary and make up new spells for Harry Potter.

The comic book drawing's a great idea. I love to draw, and the kids will join me occasionally, even more often if I get out some paints."

Deborah said, "My youngest loves to read fact and science books. Just recently he's branched into R.L. Stine, which makes his horror writer mama very pleased. Let me know if that comic book idea works on yours."

Jeff Hayes said, "Excellent post - I think you and Chloe have accomplished something wonderful."

Chris said, "Deborah: With my son, the comic thing comes and goes. I'll try again. He's the same way, science books, anything with volcanoes and weather. I don't have many comics or graphic novels, but I bought a few to try to entice him into drawing or writing one...without much success. It seems like more work than writing to me, and I like to draw. I've goofed a little with the idea of doing a graphic novel, but I don't have the doggedness. If someone had a drawing/painting version of NaNoWriMo, I wouldn't be able to do it.

"Jeff: Thanks. Today, I found myself wondering what things will be like a year from now? How many Wreaths out there? Hope there are a lot of them."

Isabelle Gissinger

The Y Logs

I'm a 26-years old French graphic-designer, who also happens to have an experience as technical writer for software manuals. As far as I can remember, I've always loved writing, especially when it comes to fiction works. However, only recently have I taken on the commitment to really write seriously, in the aim of being published, and not only for my own leisure.

Manifesto of the Point in Writing

I'm bouncing off a comment I posted earlier on, itself triggered by several posts I had read on the NaNoWriMo forums. At times, some people would ask "what did your family/friends said when you announced you were going to write a novel in one month?". And at times, some people would answer that they got told "what's the point of writing a novel if you're not going to publish it?".

Perhaps this is why there can be such a rift between authors and non-authors, artists and non-artists. As odd as it can seem to me, who love what I do both as a hobby and in the hopes of taking it onto a professional path, there are people who don't see the point of writing just for the sake of writing.

To each their own, after all (for instance, I don't really understand why someone would like cooking for hours—I don't like it much myself), but it got me thinking: back to the very core of the problem, we have absolutely NO way of knowing whether we'll get published one day. We can make all the efforts needed, undergo all the mandatory steps, but there's still no 100% certainty that our stories or illustrations someday manage to end up in the spotlight. From this point on, why bother? It's nothing sure, so why make the effort if it's not necessarily going to pay off in the end?

The answer is so simple that it's laughable: because we like it. Because these words are in us, and need to be left out sooner or later. Because worlds are born and die within our minds, and deserve a chance at existing outside there. Because we wield the pen and keyboard the same way craftspeople wield their tools. Because we feel like it.

Whether we're working on our writing with a professional aim in sight or just as a hobby, it's not a road so easy to take that someone hating writing would take it just for… what? The sake of money? Nothing's certain in the world of publication, right? Nothing tells me that I'll be the next Rowling.

Anyway, to anyone wondering why an author can write a novel without aiming at having it published, or without knowing for sure that it'll be published, here's the answer: we love writing. Simple as that. Quod erat demonstrandum.

Just like my neighbor next door loves spending three hours in a row preparing delicious dishes that will only get wolfed down in a matter of minutes. Because we like it. Because we love it.

Readers Response

Chris Howard said, "Brilliant. There's the pride in completing something as monumental as a 50k+ word novel. (71k+ in your case!) I don't care what anyone says, it's not easy. (I've had people say NaNoWriMo didn't seem that difficult). There's the progress of our art, that we get better with every story we write. I can't say this applies in every case, but I can look back on my writing and—generally speaking—I am a better writer today than yesterday. Nothing's certain in the world of publication, right? Nothing tells me that I'll be the next Rowling. Right. Rowling didn't know she was going to be the next. Barry Cunningham, who signed Harry Potter for Bloomsbury, didn't know.

"Here's a quote. I think I read this in a writing book, and it applies to writers of all genres, not just horror. I may be getting it completely wrong—so King fans correct me, but here it goes: When someone asked Stephen King why he wrote horror, he replied, "What makes you think I have a choice?" Of course, it works better with horror, but on some level it applies to all writers, right?"

Fredcq said, "I agree. I have no choice but to write. I have always had some sort of creative outlet in my life; drawing, music and so forth. I found that the one thing that I was really good at was story telling. I learned this craft from running a Role-playing game for 20 years with my friends. You tend to learn a few things about pacing and plot holes from playing RPGs. The funny thing was, I never thought that I would have the patience to write a whole book. Back then I was still playing music. I started to give writing a go when the stories that I wanted to tell were too long and complex to fit into a song.

"Great job on NANO by the way. I tried it last year but could not finish. I wiped out after two weeks. The sad part is the novel that I was working on somehow got corrupted. 23000 words down the drain. Even my back ups were bad."

Benjamin Solah said, "I can't help it!" I scream. (grin) It's inevitable. And it gives some interest to an otherwise boring life. Sure the goal is publication, but I doubt it'd be a complete waste if it didn't happen."

Yzabel said, "Chris – For me NaNo wasn't as hard as I had thought, but mainly because I had never envisioned my writing in terms of quantity (words), and was fooled by the "OMG it must be a hell of a lot!" feeling. Evidently, given that I type fast, the average 1,667 words didn't take me three hours every day. It still was more than I was used to do, in any case. Besides, I don't doubt that hadn't I had a plan for my novel, it'd all have gone down the drain very fast. As a sidenote regarding the progress of our art, I've found a few texts on paper at noon while searching other documents in the mess of my desk. I was amazed to notice that I had manage to squeeze "again" five times in two lines. Gah."

"Fredcq – That's a case of bad luck here with the NaNovel. Well, if you do it again, I hope you wont't lose it. Even if not reaching the 50k, 20-25k is still a pretty good basis to bounce off later on.

"Re: the RPG, I can only agree! It also taught me that nothing ever goes as planned, and that the 'heroes' will sooner or later come up with something incredibly clerver, risky, stupid, even (often?) or the three at the same time. The real difference I've experienced between GMing and planning a novel is that I need to know from the start where I'm headed to—when I GM, I always leave a wide margin maneuver, so that the players aren't caught within my net from beginning to end, and can do things in a more unusual way if they like.

"In fact, when I somewhat lack inspiration, I tend to convert my characters according to the rules of a game which universe is close enough (I did it for some of the chars in my WIP, taking the Cyberpunk 2020 rulebook). Then I roll the dice to see how things go. It doesn't build the story for me, but it makes certain situations go more realistic/exciting at times (even the hero can botch a Stealth or Alertness roll), and allows me to better vizualize the fights, chase scenes, etc. Moreover, it's fun to do.

"Benjamin – Indeed, life's less boring this way. (And it's not a waste of time as long as it's at least funny, even if we don't do much more with it.)"

fredcq said, "I sensed that you were a gamer but I wasn't sure. I ran Cyberpunk for a while when we are all into reading William Gibson and cyberspace. The main game that we played was the Warhammer Fantasy Roleplaying system. I liked it because it was much darker than D&D and it had a fast moving combat system.

When I first started writing, I tried to convert my Warhammer campaign into a book but it just did not work. It had a lot to do with how erratic the characters used to act. My players were really good but their behavior would not translate well into a novel. I do go back and pick out things here and there and incorporate them into my stories now and then, just because some of the ideas do work."

Yzabel said, "I'm more of a World of Darkness player/storyteller (I'm trying to adapt the Mage rules to use them for my SF/Fantasy upcoming story), but I've also tried Warhammer. That was 4-5 years ago, though, so I can't remember everything very well.

There was a time I was keeping very precise notes on a Mage campaign, in order to write the 'diary' of my character in the shape of a novel (well… several, in fact). It didn't work out because the whole group split before the end, but I'm sure it could have been great. Then I have my other group, who pulled some very funny stunts at times (including dressing as J-rock idols and descending into a Tokyo gay bar to dance naked, and, errm… yes, yes, they were mages. With power and all. * roll her eyes *) Now, there are indeed ideas who do work. Some of them I've reused as well."

Jennifer said, "Love it. Simple as that. For me it's the creativity. I love to create and by writing I can share it. By writing it comes alive. Words on a paper enable me to share the worlds in my head and there is nothing more fun than that."

Deborah said, "I started out as a voracious reader of horror and fantasy novels, much to my parents' chagrin. They thought I should read sappy romance novels like a good girl. But I was drawn to reading horror novels and wasn't a bit surprised when I started writing them. I don't think my family was surprised, either. They don't understand my compulsion to write and worried about whether or not I was obsessed. I've given up on my obsession with being a best selling novelist. Whether I become one or not doesn't matter, as long as I can keep writing."

Yzabel said, "Jennifer – Nicely put. Why keep all of this in us, if we can get it out and share it!"

"Deborah – The version I got was "you need to read 'the French classics' because they're the important books". Good thing that I did read a good deal of them, along with the SF, horror and fantasy books I read as well, at least nobody could give me the reproachful look anymore."

Deborah said, "I agree that it's a good idea to read classic literature as well as other genres, including nonfiction. It sounds like you've had a well-rounded education.

I've hardly touched the literature classics unless I was forced to for a school assignment. Edgar Rice Burroughs and Robert Heinlein were two of my classical faves."

fredcq said, "I read what I like to read. If I want to read a classic, I do. I don't like forcing myself to do something, just because it's something that I am "supposed" to do to be a better writer or a person. If a book does not hold my attention, it is very difficult for me to finish. Since I started writing, I find that I enjoy more non ficiton than fiction. Although, reading fiction helps me write better and motivates me."

Yzabel said, "Deborah – I even liked it! (grin) I used to devour novels by Emile Zola, among other things (the Rougon-Macquart saga). Later on, I switched to English classics, after we had to translate some Shakespeare in class and I thought "the results were frigging hilarious, I need to read more by myself". I know, I have weird reasons at times, but as long as they make me read…"

"Fredcq – For me, it depends on the moments. This month, for instance, I'm reading only non-fiction (and it takes me quite some time, since Dawkins' book isn't exactly a short nor an easy one). I don't know if reading classics can make me a "better" writer, but I still think it helped me in some way, especially in English. On the other hand, some classics I find utterly boring, and I'm not ashamed of saying it. Anyway, after having proclaimed that I really didn't like The Da Vinci code, I don't think anything can ashame me in that regard."

fredcq said, "I know what you mean. I have moments where I want to read stuff like Don Quixote (sp?) or Dante's Inferno. Unfortunately, I sometimes find it very hard to wade through that stuff.

I think that I may be the only person who hasn't read the Da Vinci Code. I have heard a few negative things from people who I trust so I will probably stay away. I have a whole bookshelf of unread books to get though anyway. Your english, your writing at least is very good. If your profile didn't say that you were from France, I would have never known."

Elvira Black said, "I agree—a passion for creating is what can drive a writer or any other artist to persevere against all "odds."

Yzabel said, "Ah, passion—this is the word. After all, we wouldn't go as far as to bother so much about the quality of our writing if it wasn't more than "only a hobby among others.""

Benjamin Solah
Benjamin Solah's Blog

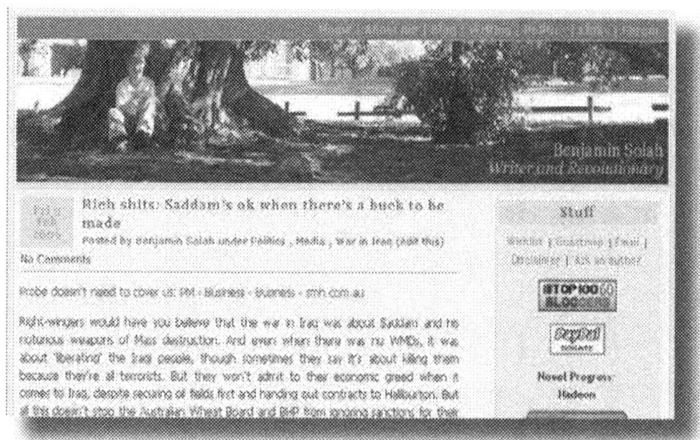

My name is Benjamin Solah, a 19 year old from Sydney, Australia. I'm a writer of dark fiction, working towards the dream of being a full-time writer. I'm also a Marxist revolutionary, who is prominent in Anti-War, Anti-Capitalist and pro-refugee campaigns.

Ask an Author: Finding Time to Write

Mike Marinaro from 'Ramblings and Rhetoric' asks: "With all of the things going on in our busy lives, how do we make the time to sit down and seriously do some writing on a regular basis?"

I think this a good question, and something I need to address for myself, and I think it is a matter of priorities. If you really want to write and be a writer, you will quite easily find the time to write. The motivation has to be there. I realise for full-time workers, this is a lot harder than students, housekeepers etc.

Before Stephen King became a well-known author, he also had a full time job, as an English Teacher. It was tough and he really didn't like it, and although he seemed swamped with it, he still found time to write. He was so determined that he used to shut himself away in the little laundry of his trailer and write. Eventually his persistence payed off, and now I'm sure, he has plenty of time to write whenever he wants.

But from personal experience, the key to finding time to write has a lot to do with shutting out distractions and procrastinating. I bet a lot of you have cursed yourself time and time again for wasting so much time surfing the net, where this time could be better spent writing. Though the Internet is a wonderful place, and you can learn so much, and meet so many new people, there is a limit to how much you should spend there if you're considering doing this writing thing seriously. TV also falls into this category. If you really want to write, 'Desperate Housewives,' will seem less important then the manuscript you've been dying to finish.

So, get your priorities straight, if writing is important enough to you, other things will seem less important. Also, a little moderation, I'm not condoning obsessive writers who spend every last second free at their word processor. I think I'd go mad. Watch movies, read books, surf the net and go for a walk, but leave some decent space for some writing too, if it is important to you.

Readers Response

Fredcq said, "At this point, I try to write during every free moment that I can. I thankfully have a small 12" laptop with a long battery life which I carry everywhere.

"Stephen King is a great inspiration to me as a writer. Besides telling great horror stories, he is one of the few multi-million selling authors who still supports the short story."

Doris said, "I think you are right - it is a matter of getting your priorities right and getting on with it. Applies to most things really! If there is a will, there is a way."

Yzabel said, "I totally agree. While I'm a Master Procrastinator myself, I'm also doing my best to learn to give myself the much needed kicks in the bottom to "work" on my writing when the motivation isn't there. (Of course, when motivated, it comes all by itself, but we all have our highs and lows, and writing isn't an exception, at least for me.) At the worst, I'll bring the laptop or a notepad in front of the TV, if really I don't want to miss; I won't be as productive, but it'll be something instead of nothing at all.

"Doing NaNoWriMo this year showed me that I could do it. The rest is now a matter of choice, and if I want to surf the web, alright, I just won't whine about "not having the time to write" after this. Although most of what I do on the web is writing in my themed blogs and leaving a few comments, anyway, so it's not *that* bad."

Carolyn said, "That's good advice and well heeded. It is far too easy to slump in front of the TV or PC and get caught up in other BS! (grin) It makes one lazy and they start writing in letter abbreviations.

"I need to buckle back down and muster some inspiration. Thanks for the reminder, Ben!"

suki said, "I think that the same goes for anything else you want to do just have to put your mind to it!"

Seawave said, "Just want to add another nod to what has already been said. Great advice, Ben. Anything that an individual has a passion for needs to be made a priority. I'm sure if we were all to sit down and think seriously about how much time is given on a daily basis to things low on our priority list, some rearrangement could certainly be made. Thanks for the great post."

Cavan said, "I like to write out everything longhand, for a number of reasons. One of them is that I'm not tempted to check my email or go blogsurfing."

Blogging a Sonnet . . . or Sonnetting a Blog?

This is a poem about my blog
The one where I rant
It'll make you as sick as a dog
And you might begin to pant

I write about writing
I write about politics
The words you are sighting
Not quite, like the classics

If you don't like this sonnet
I really don't care
I'll stick dynamite in your bonnet
Even if it isn't quite fair

This blog, I have flogged
A poem, instead of blogged

Clive Allen

Gone Away

I was born in England In 1948 but grew up in Southern Africa. I married there and we had a son, Matthew, who is now 34 years old and a web designer (he provides the technical expertise behind my website).

I live in Massachusets, and I write for Syntagma Media while I search for an agent to represent my work, in particular a book entitled *The Gabbler's Testament*.

Living Backwards

I was miles from anywhere when I first saw him. He was walking at the side of the road, gas can in hand, and I assumed that he'd run out of fuel somewhere. I didn't remember passing any stranded cars on the road but figured he could have broken down on a side road. Anyone would have stopped to give him a ride.

Because I had one of those mental debates while deciding whether or not to stop, the car was quite a distance ahead of him when I brought it to a halt. I watched in the mirror as he approached. He was in no hurry, it seemed, just ambling along as though out for a stroll. When he came level with the passenger window, I leaned over and called out to him.

"D'you need a ride to the next gas station, pal?"

He stopped and leaned over so that he could see my face.

"Actually, David, I was hoping you'd take me all the way to Akron."

I swear I'd never set eyes on the guy in my life before. How could he know my name? And the fact that I was driving to Akron? I was too dumbfounded to say anything in reply and just watched while he opened the door to get into the car. As he sat down, he threw the gas can into the bushes.

"Aren't you gonna need that?" I asked.

"Oh no, I was only carrying it so you'd take pity on me and stop," he replied. "Bought it at that gas station where you're going to drop me off. But you wouldn't have seen that, of course. You were gone by then."

This was becoming confusing. Was he claiming to have met me before or was he some kind of lunatic with wild delusions?

"Pardon?" I said. "Have we met before or something?"

"Yes and no, David. Look, it's complicated. Why don't you get this thing moving and I'll explain as we go, okay?"

I realized then that he was right. If he was a madman, the sooner I got him to where he wanted to go, the better. He didn't look dangerous or anything, in his early twenties but slightly built and pale, as if he'd been locked away out of the sunlight. I could easily win any tussle with him, I figured. So he wanted to talk in riddles? That was fine; it might be amusing and help the journey to go that much faster. I eased the stick into Drive and let the car move off.

"How d'you know my name?" I asked as we reached the speed limit and I hit the cruise control.

"You told me," he replied. When I said nothing but raised one eyebrow a little, he continued, "I'd better explain from the beginning. As I said before... Oh, you won't remember that, of course. Fact is, David, I'm living backwards."

A dim memory sparked in my brain. "You mean like Merlin? I read a book once by T.H. White about him. Called *The Once and Future King*, I think. Anyway, it was about King Arthur and all that but I remember Merlin was supposed to be living backwards in it. Is that what you mean?"

"Exactly," he said.

I waited for him to go on but he said no more; just sat there watching my reaction to his ridiculous statement. So I gave him none.

"Am I supposed to believe that?" I asked. "It's a pretty freaky thing to say, you know."

He laughed. "Yup, it's weird alright. Most people would be driving me to the loony bin by now. But that's why I chose you. You're going to believe me by the time we get to Akron."

I don't often snort but I did so then. This guy was a hoot. "Okay, pal, tell me more. I'll listen."

"We'd better get that sorted for a start. I'm not your pal, well, not yet anyway. My name's Merlin."

This time I couldn't hide my disbelief. I turned and looked at him. "Are you serious? Are you trying to tell me that you're *the* Merlin?"

"That's me," he said, without blinking an eye. "Old Merlin the magician, alive and well in the 21st Century, living backwards and loving it. Quite a kicker, huh?"

I couldn't help but smile. "You're crazy," I said. "Pretty entertaining, I grant you, but crazy as a loon."

He grinned back at me. "Yup, you're right. Nutty as a fruitcake, that's me. But that's got nothing to do with what we're talking about. I'm still living backwards."

There was a sincerity in his voice that stopped me from dropping him off right there and then. Crazy he may have been but I couldn't help liking the guy. I decided to play along and see how good his story was.

"So, okay, you reckon you're Merlin. But how can that be? He lived, oh, about fifteen hundred years ago, I reckon. How could you be that old? Look at you, you're no more than twenty-five at the most."

"Ah," he said, "That's the thing, you see. I'm living backwards so I'm younger now than I was then."

"But more than a thousand years? Come on, even living backwards you're not going to be born for a millennium at least."

"Always with the math," he sighed and eased himself back into the seat to watch the road ahead. "It's hard to understand, David, but basically it's like swimming against the tide. Easy enough for you folks just going with the flow; of course you live much faster. But for me it's a struggle. Takes me three hundred years to get ten years older."

I did some quick mental calculations. That would make him about seventy in Arthur's time; about right, I thought. And it also meant...

"So you're not going to be born for another six hundred years?"

"You catch on fast," he said.

There was silence for a long time then. I was trying to think of a way to catch him out and he seemed content to wait. The mid west hurtled by our windows.

Eventually, I thought I had sorted things out and was ready for him again.

"So, to you, the future is like the past? You can remember what's going to happen?"

"Yup," he said.

"And the past is like the future?"

"Just so," he returned.

I thought I had him then. "Ah, in that case, how can you know about King Arthur? How can you make jokes about being the great magician when you can't possibly know that's what he was?"

It was his turn to snort. "Oh come on, David; you can do better than that. I can read, can't I? D'you think we don't have books in the future? And, as it happens, I've read Mallory and that guy White you mentioned. Which reminds me..."

"What?" I asked.

"Oh, nothing. Was just thinking that I might drop in on old T.H. in a few years and give him some ideas."

"So now you're the reason he wrote that book?" This was becoming weird. "I suppose you created all our history on your way back to 500 AD?"

"Nah, don't be silly," he said. "Just think I might dabble a bit here and there."

"Oh great. Now we've got a lunatic running around in history, tweaking and fiddling."

He laughed again. "Hey, don't get worried. It's all past to you and anything I do is already incorporated."

We fell silent again as I pondered this. Then he began to speak and I just listened.

"You see, David, six hundred years from now we're going to be able to do things that you can't even dream of. Look at the pace of change over the last hundred years or so. It's accelerating all the time. In a few hundred years we're going to prove that time travel is impossible. But we're also going to find a way to turn ourselves around and live in the opposite direction. Not that many will, of course. In fact, I'm the only one. But it's a form of time travel, I suppose."

He paused to see how I'd react to this. Once again, I didn't. So he went on.

"We became aware that there was something that needed doing in the past. And I volunteered. I've always liked history and I wanted to see it for myself. To actually make a contribution to it was an unbelievable dream.

"It's slow, of course. Man, you can't imagine how slow it is. But it's the only way we've got. All to do with changes at the molecular level, you know."

He rambled on into a long explanation of how it worked but I couldn't understand it. He probably knew that but was just enjoying the opportunity to speak. And I turned everything over in my mind as I drove. It was all too much to be believed but he certainly made a pretty airtight story of it. His knowledge of my name and destination was hard to explain away especially. And that strange business of the gas can.

By the time we got to Akron, night had fallen. Merlin directed me through the dark streets towards the gas station and it occurred to me that he seemed to know his way around pretty well.

"You've been here before, haven't you?" I asked.

"Nope. Just remember it from the future. Take a left here."

"I'm sorry but I can't believe that."

He glanced at me then. "Okay, Mr Doubtful, get your head round this. When we get to the gas station there'll be a green

SUV filling up. The driver's a young blonde woman in jeans and a pink top. And just after we arrive, a silver Honda will drive in from the opposite direction."

It was just as he said. I stopped the car and began to apologize for my doubts but he shrugged them off. "It's okay, David, I get it all the time. Thanks for the ride, by the way."

A thought crossed my mind then. "Oh, uh, Merlin, you said you chose me as your ride. Why was that?"

He winked. "Figure of speech. Actually I just traced you back from this moment."

He opened the door and was getting out when I realized that there was something else I wanted to know.

"And what about Arthur and all that?" I asked. "What was it that you have to change?"

He turned to look at me. For a moment he seemed to be considering something, as though he wasn't sure that I could be trusted with it, but then he shrugged and spoke.

"That Arthur thing wasn't it at all," he said. "It was just one of my little tweaks. After all, we know the Angles and Saxons win in the end, don't we?"

There was a slight pause before he went on. "No, after Arthur, I'm going to wander over to Persia. There's a couple of interesting guys there that I want to meet and get to know. And then, just before I die, the three of us have an appointment in a stable in a little town called Bethlehem..."

He turned away. The last I saw of him was a slight and unimposing figure walking into the bright lights of the service station.

Readers Response

Trée said, ""Always with the math," A gem of a phrase if ever there was one. Beautiful Clive."

keeefer said, "What an excellent tale. Most enjoyable Mr. Gone. Would a baby Merlin be able to magic his soiled nappy clean? And what would he use as a pacifier.... Babies with magical powers, there's gotta be a hollywood film script in there somewhere."

Gone Away said, "Thanks, Trée, glad you liked it. But weren't Merlin's apparently magical powers just the technological tricks of a much later age, Keef? And think of the fortune you could make on the horses! Easy to make predictions when it was just yesterday to you."

Twelvebirds said, "Oh, what a wonderful tale, although I must admit the concept of living backwards has my head spinning. I hadn't thought about the magical powers simply being tricks of the future until I read that comment. It makes sense and fits so well with the Merlin character. I think I am far too linear to get it all straight in my head, what with going backward but ending up forward, or vice versa. A great story but I have one question. Which of the three Wise Men was he?"

Gone Away said, "Good question, Twelve - just been wondering that myself. At a guess, I'd have to say Melchior, if only because it starts with the same letter and just might be a corruption of Merlin..."

Mark Pettus said, "As Jesu helpe hym for hys grete myght, as he is the servaunt of Jesu bothe day and nyght. I don't know. It just seemed fitting."

Gone Away said, "Well, dang, Mark - ya got me both ways with that. As a Christian and as a sucker for anything Olde English. It's fitting alright.

"Great blog, by the way. Shall have to find time to add it to the blogroll. Found it a few times but keep losing it. Good luck in the new job, especially trying to write as well; I never found a way to do that..."

Autumn said, "Oh my! That was just wonderful, thoroughly enjoyed every aspect, not least the fact that my mind is now doing dizzying cartwheels."

Gone Away said, "Thank you, Autumn. It's an interesting concept, isn't it?"

keeefer said, "Happy 200th blog, by the way."

Gone Away said, "Thanks, Keef. (grin)"

Mad said, "I really enjoyed that!"

Gone Away said, "Makes a change, does it, Mad?"

Mad said, "Just the kind of thing I enjoy, Dad."

Gone Away said, "Just joshin', Mad."

Dr Callahan said, "What a great story! May I have permission to use it on a blog giving you credit of course. Thank you, Dennis O' Callaghan"

Gone Away said, "Thank you, Dennis (may I call you Dennis - oh, I just did, didn't I?). My feeling is that anything I put in the blog is out there on the net for anyone to read and use. So of course you may borrow it. But give me a link, won't you? And here's to the Emerald Isle!"

keeefer said, "I got to pondering last eve and I was going to post this on my blog. However, those that visit my pages tend to be on the younger side of life and I think this question requires an older slant. I am a firm believer that when one gets older that person inherits wisdom (along with senility). So please, if you can keep your venerable mind on the matter, can you tell me why we have the phrase 'A pair of trousers'? I did think that maybe it was because there are two legs, but a shirt has 2 arms and we don't have a pair of shirts. Can you please enlighten me, oh forgetful one, on this delightful anomaly of language."

Mad said, "Ooooh! I know, I know! It's because early pantaloons were in two parts, basically two legs that were tied together at their tops around your waist. So at one time it really was a pair of pants."

Gone Away said, "Sorry, what was the question? Oh, yes. Well, I think you'll find that way back in the mists of time, trousers were invented as a form of leg warmer that slipped over your legs. The unmentionables were covered by a loincloth, probably. So you always had two trousers, otherwise you'd have had one warm leg and one blue. Then someone had the brilliant idea of attaching the trousers to the loincloth - voila! The pair of trousers were born.

"All of this is pure conjecture, of course, but it ought to be good enough to fool your young friends, Keef. Come to think of it, it's an exact parallel to the development of the pantyhose..."

keeefer said, "Now thats what I thought but having limited knowledge of Pre 1900's Menswear I thought I'd best get a second opinion. So why do we have a pair of pants then was their originally a loincloth per testicle?"

Gone Away said, "One more thought on the matter (having read Mad's comment - he's right, of course). It all sounds perfectly sensible until one remembers that Roman soldiers wore trousers under their battledress. They didn't call them trousers (perhaps they were pantums) but certainly they were a dead ringer for what we call trousers today (admittedly cut off just below the knee). So who really invented the system? And don't say Pantus Trouserus..."

Gone Away said, "The word "pants" comes from "pantaloons", obviously. And Mad has explained about them. However, I would like to offer the following alternative theory: Some bright spark had the idea of cutting off the trousers very close to the nether regions, thus creating short trousers or what are sometimes known as shorts. He noticed that the ladies' tended to breath a little quicker at sight of a nicely-turned male leg and jokingly began to refer to them as "pants" therefore. Offered in all seriousness. Almost."

Keeefer said, "Apparently the Phrygians made trousers too whilst the greeks wore Chitons (which was evidently a reference to the state of the clothing due to the lack of toilet roll available "oh look he's got chiton his clothing again')"

Gone Away said, "And, of course, the Phrygians invented them because they sick of people calling them Phrigids as they were always cold (Phrygia is in what is now known as Russia)."

keeefer said, "Ahhhh, hence why they needed those iron curtains."

Kate said, "That was wicked! It's really good, I mean. Thanks for posting it."

Gone Away said, "Thanks, Kate, I'm glad you liked it. And, even though I'm ancient, I do know what "wicked" means these days!"

Raven Ridesemraw said, "Wow! That was fantastic!"

Phish said, "If you could go back in time then why not hit all the hot spots of history? Very interesting that he ended up as wise and magical figures. Very imaginative. The comment thread about the pants was hilarious. Both the post and the comments here are always a good read."

Gone Away said, "Glad you enjoyed it, Raven."

Gone Away said, "Thanks, Phish. I have always found White's concept of living backwards to be quite fascinating; the possibilities are almost endless. And, as for the comment thread, well, methinks my commenters should take a bow!"

Marti said, "Wonderful story! Best wishes for a happy Thanksgiving to you and your family!"

Gone Away said, "Thank you, Marti! And I trust that you and yours will have a wonderful Thanksgiving too."

Janus said, "Very good and very original, I wish I could age backwards at times."

Gone Away said, "Thanks, Janus. Me, I think I'll stick with aging forwards. At least there's an end in sight going this way..."

Scot said, "Clive, Oh, my, how you so digress from past to future and then end very present. But then again, sometimes we have to live backwards to discover the magic of who we are now. I loved how you set this up, and kept me reading out of curiosity to see where you were going. Nice."

Gone Away said, "Thanks, Scot. If you liked it, I know I've done my job."

Humor and Humour

Let's face it, humor and humour are two different things. Although the Americans and the British can understand many of each other's jokes, there are areas of comedy where one nation will stare at the other in blank incomprehension. Yet both have specialties (specialities) in which they excel and there is some sharing of television comedy shows between the two nations.

A few British TV shows make it all the way across the Atlantic without amendment; *Monty Python's Flying Circus* and *The Benny Hill Show* spring to mind. And both of these examples are interesting in that they represent the adolescent side of Brit humor, the sort of surreal jokes that schoolboys or university students make in their wilder moments.

Does this mean that the Americans are only able to appreciate a simpler, zany sort of humor? I think not for, when we look at American comedies, we find a degree of sophistication that destroys that theory. It is much more that the slapstick element in the two shows mentioned is a common language between many cultures, a comedic language that is easily understood by almost everyone. Why, even *Mr. Bean* (cringe) succeeded in America.

Notice that generally American shows can be imported into Britain without editing and that there are far more of them than those that make the crossing in the other direction. I can think of several straight away: *WKRV, Taxi, Seinfeld, Everybody Loves Raymond, Friends*. The list is almost endless and they are all sitcoms, a genre that the Brits still mistakenly imagine that they do best.

The British sitcom is an awful creature, rarely funny and unremittingly depressing. Just occasionally, a Brit sitcom will sneak into America under the auspices of PBS. *Keeping Up Appearances* is one that I've seen over here; it has a small American following but I merely find it irritating and embarrassing, probably because it's just too close to the truth to be funny.

The fact is that Americans do sitcom far better than the Brits. There is a surrealistic quality to their best offerings that ought to be present in British sitcoms but never is. We fill our sitcoms with the old guard of acting and give them lines to read that we think are sophisticated but turn out to be merely obvious. Surrealism we leave to Monty Python.

So the Brits do not find it necessary to change American sitcoms in any way; we happily accept and understand them. It's the game shows that we decide need to be changed to suit our market and there are any number of British copies of American inventions in this genre.

The Americans, however, have the good sense to leave Brit game shows very much alone (can you imagine an American Pot Black?) but will sometimes take a British comedy show and attempt to produce an American version. A while ago I saw an attempt to Americanize Fawlty Towers and it was, frankly, awful. Some producer had failed to realize that the essential ingredient to the show was always going to be John Cleese.

On rare occasions, this type of American import has some measure of success. Archie Bunker of *All In The Family* is an example, although I doubt many Americans realize that he is a copy of Alf Garnet from *Till Death Do Us Part*. Yet so much is lost in the translation; Archie falls way short of the abrasive, unrelenting, cutting sharpness of Alf. And this illustrates the reason for America wanting to copy some Brit shows rather than allow them air time in the States: sometimes British humor is just too harsh and vicious for general consumption.

I suppose that the differences in the two nations' sense of humor has come about partly through development over the last two centuries but also because America has had the injection of so many different nationalities, each with its own brand of humor.

Some years ago a friend of mine married a lady from Sweden and went to live there. On one of his return visits to England he confessed to me that he did not understand the Swedish sense of humor. Apparently they would find quite ordinary events hilarious but, when he tried English jokes on them, he'd be met with blank stares. Of course, as an Englishman, my natural response was amazement that the Swedes had a sense of humor at all, but the story does show that the Americans and British are not so far apart in their understanding of comedy. In just some areas there is a lack of comprehension.

As an instance of this, I find no equivalent in America of the British love of wordplay. This is something so natural to the Brits that it often occurs in the course of ordinary conversation. Certain words seem to be catalysts for it; "chicken" is probably the most likely to start off a rapid exchange of silly sentences:

"He had chickens in the back garden, you know."
"Really? And no-one sent him up before the beak?"
"Nah, that would have been a poultry thing to do."
"Well I wasn't going to lay down the law about it."

"Eggzactly. Not something to brood over at all."

"Yes, if a feller wants to feather his nest, why try to coop him up?"

"Flocked if I know..."

That sort of conversation just doesn't happen in the States. I've tried to start them but people just look at me as if I'm weird. And I suppose it is a strange way to get a laugh, to build an impromptu competition for the snappiest pun.

I just miss it sometimes, that's all...

Readers Response

John (SYNTAGMA) said, "It's always said that Americans don't do irony. You put your finger on why. Irony is so subtle it can easily be taken literally, with disastrous results. With so many nationalities there, you can't afford to be subtle, you have to spell it out for fear of misunderstandings. Alas, the same thing is happening here. British humour is not what it was.

Mad said, "I will agree that most Brit sitcoms are awful but occasionally they get it just right. "Red Dwarf" and "My Family" spring to mind.

"It is also true that Brit humour can be very vicious, something I hadn't thought about until recently. From "The Office" (which I find too painful to watch) to Brit humour in the work place the twist of the knife adds the element of danger that can be hilarious.

"As for the Swedes? I love 'em. My Swedish friends Rolf and Paula think I'm hilarious which I heartily enjoyed. I didn't even have to do anything funny, they just thought I was... actually thinking about the Thai's think I'm funny too.

"(I can live without the pun game however)"

Gone Away said, "Never tell that to an American, John. They do irony, it's just that they do it so well it shoots above our heads.

"That's the strange thing I found when I was writing this - on both sides of the Atlantic there are times when there is great subtlety in humor and others where we descend to slapstick. But it's in the choice of when these things are appropriate that the difference comes. Much misunderstanding results from one other side resorting to subtlety when the other is least expecting it."

Gone Away said, "Red Dwarf is an exception mainly because it's Monty Python meets Blake Seven. I never saw My Family and wish I'd never even heard of The Office (seriously unfunny). The fact that the Americans have done a copy of The Office is completely incomprehensible to me.

"But I can see how it must be gratifying to get a whole nation laughing without exerting oneself at all. It might worry me a bit if they kept on laughing, however..."

Mad said, "I've often wondered if I could've been a mega famous comedian in Thailand..."

ME Strauss said, "You have hit on something there, Clive in using the word *when*. We Americans have our puns and our subtle dry humor, but I've found that we use it at totally different times. We're all for comic relief on one hand and find it totally in appropriate on the other. Often it depends which group you are in.

"My experience is that our version of the 'pun game' is more of a game of verbal volleyball, as in this exchange. When I met my (shorter) husband I asked my friend, Kathy, the bartend to get 'the little guy a drink.' He questioned that. I went over to stand beside him. He looked at my long, narrow feet and said, "Do you ski?""

Gone Away said, "Mad: What's the pay like? That is really funny, Liz, and illustrates the point of this article very well. That exchange could never have happened in Britain! I shouldn't say this but I can't resist the temptation: Your shorter husband? Where was the taller one at the time?"

Josh said, "Last of the Summer Wine is a completely unexplainable favorite of mine. I identify with Clegg; don't ask me why."

Gone Away said, "I agree, Josh; Last of the Summer Wine has a strong attraction, perhaps because it's humor is gentle and inoffensive. And everyone wants to be Clegg - the observer, not quite as insane as the others but willing to travel with them...

Kurt said, "Perhaps it's the company I keep, or the fact that I live among a bunch of honors university students, but I've never found a lack of wordplay among the circles I travel in here. In fact, exchanges like the one above occur at the very least several times weekly. Perhaps Clive should be spending more time with the younger crowd?"

Gone Away said, "Perhaps indeed, Kurt. I confess that this was an "angling post", some bait laid out to see whether the art of wordplay is still alive and flourishing in some corner of America. You have given me new hope if it survives amongst the students, at least!"

Beltane said, "I could just wallow away in Brit humor all day long and be delightfully happy. One of my favorite drama shows is Spooks (they call it MI-5 in the states, it airs on A&E). I think the thing I love about Brit humor the most is the wordplay, the intelligence of it and the dryness. I think it's really the dryness that goes over most Americans heads. For the average American, Dumb and Dumber really was the pinnacle. *sigh* While I do get a kick out of toilet humor when in the mood, it's not our best example."

Gone Away said, "Ah yes, Beltane, we do like our humor dry and delivered with a poker face. But there is good American comedy around too, much better Dumb and Dumber. I can watch Seinfeld repeats until I know them off by heart..."

Autumn said, "Wonderfully comprehensive post! The chicken dialogue brought about the giggles. Other people's humour is the hardest reaction of all to understand."

Gone Away said, "Yes indeed, Autumn. And the worst thing of all is to try to explain a joke to someone who doesn't understand!"

John said, "You are so spot on Clive, great post, and I loved the joke, must tell it at Church on Sunday!"

Gone Away said, "Nothing like a good pun, hey, John."

Stuart said, "There is much that mystifies me about America Clive, not just the humour. Take the Croc Hunter for example - many Australians think he's a complete idiot and yet the Americans love him. And the true professional croc hunters here in Australia can't work out why the crocs haven't eaten him yet. Perhaps its because he makes crocs feel rather safe."

Gone Away said, "Ah, the Croc Hunter, now you're talking! I think the reason for his popularity here is similar to stock car racing. Much as everyone watches that in the hopes that there'll be a huge pile up, the Croc Hunter is fascinating because we keep hoping he'll make a mistake and get eaten..."

keeefer said, "Another great post Gone you are on a roll. The whole things buttered me up nicely. Anyway I can't loaf about here I have some learning to do, crumbs is that the time. Still I'm glad I managed to sandwich this in between modules."

Gone Away said, "You were never one to slice things too thinly, Keef. It comes of being so well-bread, I suppose. But filling your time with reading and commenting upon my blog is no picnic, as I'm sure you know. Too much of that and you're toast!"

keeefer said, "I hadn't thought of that . . . Doh!"

Gone Away said, "(There he goes, the flour of his generation...)"

keeefer said, "Enough of your half baked comments. You need a bap on the head. Although there may be a grain of truth in it. How long can we grind this one out?"

Gone Away said, "As long as the wind turns the windmill. You don't think I'd rise to that, do you? This is more than I knead. I've half a mind to batter you about the ears. That'll get you browned off, I'm sure."

keeefer said, "You want a pizza me? Well do ya?"

Gone Away said, "That one's a bit corny, you know. Spreading it on a bit thick, I might say. You'll be wanting jam on it next..."

keeefer said, "Maybe I've bitten off a bit more than I can chew. Well now we have sorted the wheat from the chaff I hope your appetite for this type of comedy has been sated."

Gone Away said, "Well, I am replete. I'll not give you a good threshing after all. But remember for next time: I'm a crusty old soul."

keeefer said, "You may be a crusty old soul but your eyes are just glazed over."

Gone Away said, "Comes from raisin Cain..."

keeefer said, "I hope thats not sour grapes."

Delmonti said, "Hmmm.... The Americans can never, NEVER come close to these new BBC sitcoms. Extras Nighty Night"

Glenni said, "I know they are ancient now but what about "The Good Life" and 'As time goes by" I agree, Spooks is a great show and Inspector Morse, too bad he carked it! Yeah those word games were a bit . . . well you know, Anyhow great reading for one who is 'gone.'"

vanessa said, "Interesting topic. There is indeed a big difference between American and British comedy, but let's not forget about canada either;) Wow. How do I say anything here without it being misconstrued? I'm fearful I'll get backlash but here goes.... The truth of the matter is, Canadians and the Brits both share a love of self-deprecating humour. I think it's in the water. Sure it's fun to make fun of someone else, but it's always funnier to make fun of yourself. Generally speaking, Americans just don't get that. They don't like to make fun of themselves, just others. It's all fair game here though. Did that sound anti-American? It wasn't,

I assure you. I pass no judgments, it's purely observation. Oh, and yay. I *had* to throw that in. I couldn't live myself if I didn't. Thank you for that."

Gone Away said, "Ah, Dave (Delmonti), I'm glad you came by - I had entirely forgotten to revisit your blog and expound at great length upon the crane fly. I love your blog, by the way - there's just something so cool about it. How's the hip?

"As for new Brit sitcoms, are they still churning them out? Hardly worth the trouble, I'd have thought. Still, I suppose it keeps the same old faces in a job..."

Gone Away said, "Well, Glenni, Spooks I've never seen but the other two you mention are typical of what I'm talking about - vehicles for has-been actors to keep pulling the money in."

Gone Away said, "Canada, Vanessa? That's rather an obscure subject, isn't it? But seriously, I agree that the Canadians seem to have a lot in common with the Brits, although I wasn't aware that this extended to their sense of humor. They make some weird cartoons, however..."

Kitty said, "I like the post. I can see you've got sense of humor, hehe. Apart from Canada, let's not forget about Australia too. Aussies are more sarcastic in their humor I reckon."

Gone Away said, "Thanks, Kitty. I think I like Australian humor more than anyone else's - it is nothing if not direct!

Mad said, "Difference between a pot of yogurt and Australia? Left out of the fridge the yogurt will develop a culture. I'll... get my coat."

Gone Away said, "You're a brave man, Mad!"

Mad said, "I shall hide behind my online anonymity!"

Gone Away said, "And a wise one!"

Beltane said, "Bah, I love the Croc Hunter not becuase I want to see if he's eaten - but because of his enthusiasm and his genuine love of animals - and I'll admit, his derring do. He's very brave, and that's always attractive to watch and enjoy. I know some Aussies, and yeah, he's silly a bit to them, but honestly, there is nothing wrong with the guy!"

Gone Away said, "And, Beltane, as we all know, croc wrestling is a national sport in Australia!"

Yzabel said, "Interesting topic... should I say "as usual"? The very first time I saw British humour in action was through the Benny Hill shows, but I think I'd better leave them aside here, since they were a) translated in French and b) I was 7-8, and very likely just too young to understand anything. Later on, our English teacher in high school decided that we had to watch a few movies and sketches of the Monty Pythons, and I fell over laughing.

"She used to call that and "understatement" kind of humour, although I'm not sure the word is fully appropriate. Now, let me tell you that many French people absolutely don't understand it (in fact, American's seem to work better here, and I'm not sure it's just a matter of good translations). Among all my friends, I'm the only one who's ever laughed at the yoghurt-looking aliens turning British people into Scottish ones so that they could win the Wimbledon tournament (I love this sketch).

"I dig out Red Dwarf, too. Either I'm totally weird or a British-born person in the body of a French one. As a sidenote, I indeed see hwo the quoted conversation is funny.

In France, this kind of things don't work very well, though--or should I say, they work when written, but speech just doesn't convey them well."

Gone Away said, "That's interesting, Yzabel - are you saying that puns work in print in French but not in speech? Puns in English are always better when spoken..."

keeefer said, "Goscinny and Uderzo (hope they are spelt right) use a lot of wordplay humour in their Asterix books. Yet the only French performer that leaps to mind is Marcel Marceau........If French humour doesn't work when spoken then maybe he was trying to tell us something after all.

Gone Away said, "Umm yes, Keef... (is in awe at Keef's ability to spell Goscinny and Uderzo correctly)"

Mad said, "Don't be fooled he looked it up on Google."

Gone Away said, "(Hehehehe)"

keeefer said, "If I looked it up on google I'd have probably got some bizarre porn site or their 1967 tax returns."

Gone Away said, "(The man has a point...)"

Ashley said, "I must be one of the few Americans that enjoys the exchange of puns. I'm so out of practice now that I'm sure I'd never win any contest with a Brit, though I do take my small joys where I can. My husband just gives me an odd look and ignores it. *sigh*"

English Comedy vs. American Comedy said, "American's wouldn't know the real meaning of 'Comedy' if it bit them on the ass! WKRV, Taxi, Seinfeld, Everybody Loves Raymond, and Friends makes for rather dull T.V. (Please note: Have fallen asleep watching Seinfeld because it wasn't funny). Fawlty Towers staring John Cleese makes American comedy seem somewhat amateurish in comparison. I love to laugh. You 'Yanks' should try it sometime."

keeefer said, "Seems a bit harsh to me. American comedy influences English comedy quite heavily. If you look at the anarchic comedy of the Marx Brothers then compare it to the goon show the influences on people like Milligan, sellers etc are quite clear. It is from these roots that Dudley Moore and Peter Cooke draw their influences who in turn inspire Monty Python. To dismiss American humour so readily is very naive. Besides any country that can re-elect Bush is surely capable of a level of sarcastic humour far beyond us Brits."

Gone Away said, "Well, it seems there are still some Americans out there who enjoy a good pun, Ashley, so you're not alone! And I beg to differ, ECVAC. In my humble estimation, Seinfeld is the funniest show that's been on TV for years. But I guess one man's meat is another man's poison... And it seems immigrant Ozzies know a thing or two about sarcasm too, Keef."

Gary said, "We used to get "Faulty Towers" here on PBS, and I thought that was pretty good. Of course, it had John Cleese and he's very popular here. Your wordplay is what we call puns here, the lowest form of humor. Actually, right here in Austin we have the annual O'Henry Museum Pun Off. Two contestants are given a category like, for example, "meat." And then the word butchers take turns serving up lean phrases containing some meat reference. If either of the meatballs can't grind out a pun, he or she is trimmed off and chucked out and the remaining hot dog moves on to the next chopping block where the steaks are higher."

Gary said, "I just realized it was "Fawlty Towers." More wordplay."

keeefer said, "Gary, 'Your wordplay is what we call puns here, the lowest form of humor' that's certainly a bone of contention."

Yzabel said, "That's interesting, Yzabel - are you saying that puns work in print in French but not in speech? Puns in English are always better when spoken... I'm not a specialist at French humour myself--well, alright, to be honest, our comedians simply don't make me laugh very often, so I also don't watch them often--but indeed, I don't find it very... easy to make puns work in speech. Perhaps this is due to spelling and pronunciation: often, to make a pun work, we'd need to insist heavily on the spelling, which makes it awkward if thrown in in a conversation. Keeefer mentioned the Asterix example, which I find illustrates it well enough. Reading the books is hilarious, and the puns work very well, but as soon as you try to read them out loud, they seem to just fall flat, and it's "not the same anymore".

"Going to give an example here that I find pretty lame, but that illustrates the point: there's an old, old pun that goes as follows: "Comment vas-tu... yau de poêle". It can't be rendered at all by a translation, though. Basically, the pun works on "Comment vas-tu" (How are you) and the word "tuyau de poêle" (stovepipe), since once sentence ends with "tu" and the other beings with the same syllable. Written, it's easy to understand, albeit not very funny, I think. Spoken, it's not the same at all, since the word "tuyau" is normally pronounced "tu-i-o", and not "tu-yo" (if this makes sense--drats, I suck at phonetics, sorry). As said, the pun is lame anyway, but it falls even flatter when spoken.

"And now, everyone here will know how French humour can really suck."

Mad said, "Wow, your local comedy club must be a riot Yzabel..."

glenniah said, "Speaking of turf and fields, reminds me of fielding which makes me think that if the Brits are taking the Ashes away from the best cricket team in the world (TAKE NOTE MAD, Im looking for you *grin*), then they don't have much time to be concerned with comedy. Mind you, that "Freddie" Flintoff is a bit of a comedian in his own way. I wonder if Seinfeld would be interested in him."

Mad said, ""Best team in the world"? Tish pshaw, that tiny little urn Freddie was waving about says we're the best regardless of ranking..."

Gone Away said, "Gary: Well, well, once again I'm proved wrong by an American. That was a pretty meaty answer; no need to beef it up at all. And, to me, funnier than Mutton Jeff!

Gone Away said, "Yzabel: I learned French for too many years at school but have got to admit that it's still Greek to me."

Gone Away said, "Glenniah: As I recall it, the Ashes are supposed to be the ashes of English cricket, produced on the first occasion Australia beat them. In which case, they belong to us anyway..."

vanessa said, "Keef, I believe the saying goes... a pun is the lowest form of humour, unless you thought of it yourself."

Gone Away said, "I was always told that sarcasm is the lowest form of wit. The pun, however, is an entirely different art form."

Mad said, "Awwww, ain't Candians nice."

Gone Away said, "Every single one of them, Mad."

Yzabel said, "Mad: Heh. When I said we suck at humour, I wasn't... joking. Clive: Told you that it couldn't really be translated, but don't worry, it wasn't even funny to start with, so if it remains Greek to you, no biggie."

Gone Away said, "I wanted to add something about being a Dutchman if I could understand it, Yzabel, but I thought it might suffer in the translation..."

vanessa said, "Nice? NICE? Sheesh, you must be talking about the wrong country my friend. I mean, you JERK!

"Did I ever tell you I once sent 10 puns to a friend in hopes of cheering them up. Didn't work. No pun in ten did."

Gone Away said, "Groan.... All right, we're even, Vanessa."

vanessa said, "A groan is the highest compliment for a pun is it not?"

Mad said, "(She's just soooo nice)"

Gone Away said, "Indeed so, Vanessa - All mine are met by groans."

vanessa said, "Good! Just checkin'"

"Bubs, do you want me to come over there and hit you with my beavertail? It may take awhile... the snowmobile needs to warm up. Yep, yep, we're just chock full of maple-y goodness. (You are soooo jealous, I can tell...)"

M.E. Strauss
Letting Me Be

Liz Strauss has worked in print, software, and online publishing. As VP and Publisher for an American publishing company, Liz developed products with publishers in Europe, Australia, the UK and Ireland. Her personal blog is known for its originality and a writing voice inspires readers to join her as she wonders about crayons, writing, and things that don't fit. Her storytelling has a unique way of bringing others along with her on her imaginations and taking them back to their own memories.

Walking on Water

I thought I needed thinking. Time. A place to spread my mind, room for my soul.

I had read about a trucker who would drive two states away when he had things on his mind. He'd sit at a picnic table by the Mississippi River for as along as he needed to and when he was ready, he'd drive home again. I didn't have a picnic table by the Mississippi River, but I had my car and plenty of music to take me wherever I needed to go.

It had been a long week.

Some weeks are longer than others. The ones with Monday holidays seem longer for some reason. This five-day week was longer yet. The five days, for all that had to and did get done, seemed to drag and fly at the same time, and yet I didn't seem to be part of it. I didn't seem to be a part of anything. I just overachieved my way through it. How long would I do this?

I wanted to ask everyone, "What do you want from me? I can't walk on water."

I gathered a few things. I put my wallet in my back pocket, grabbed a jacket just in case, and closed the door behind me. I walked down to my little blue car, put the key in the ignition, and drove west. It was morning when I left. I had no place to go, nowhere I had to be. I'd let my car and the roads decide. I didn't want to pick.

The movement of the wheels on the road was in time with the music. The city falling further away in my rearview mirror, I got lighter by the mile. Maybe it wasn't thinking that I needed. Maybe I had done too much thinking already.

I pulled off to the side. Unclicked the latches to the top and pushed it back. Top down, now I had the sky along with me for the ride.

As the sun moved west with me, my posture softened. The music got more joyful. I started noticing how lovely the trees looked on this last "sort of warm" fall day. Memories of childhood things were floating in my mind like kids whispering.

I stopped for a late lunch at Nick's diner. Lunch was a chocolate milkshake, an old-fashioned hamburger with ketchup, mustard, pickles, onion, and ordinary—the good kind of ordinary—French fries. They were served by a woman named Doris. We talked about old-time root beer stands and real hot fudge sundaes. She was my entertainment for an hour and thirty-seven minutes. When I was done she pointed me in a new direction. I'll probably never forget her. Doris was my friend.

About two hours down the road that Doris spoke of, I found it. Boy, it was worth driving for. The sky, the sun, the water were waiting just for me. I eased off the road. I love that sound of tires on mulchy ground. I stopped the car, turned off the ignition, and just stared for a while. I grabbed my leather journal and went to find myself.

An old wooden crate sat there in the perfect spot to watch the sun and write. How it happened to be the only one and just my size, I'm not about to question. I sat down and pulled up the world.

It's nice to have the world in front of me instead of on my shoulders. It's hard to see how lovely the planet is when you bear the weight of it. I wrote that in my journal as I watched the sunset.

I thought of the ways I weigh myself down with heavy thoughts and drama. It's like covering me with so much oil. I shook off that greasy thought and set aside my journal. Instead I watched the sky change color—glorious tints of blues and grays and lavenders moving back from pinks and oranges and yellows. I felt so much room for me. I wished I could bring people here every time they asked what art meant, . . . or simplicity, . . . or elegance, . . . or peace. Yeah peace. Peace backlit with joy. Now there's a definition of elegant simplicity.

The sunset sent a beam across the water home to me. That image of a trail of light brought my day's journey back to mind. I had left home feeling broken, beat-up, and defeated. Now I believed that I could step out on that path of light and walk on water to the sun. The magic of a sunset can cure an aching heart, can still a restless mind.

I stayed until the path of light had faded into the water. Then my dream had run away with the sun to places people do not go.

I gathered up my things. I touched the crate one last time and looked out at the water under the starry sky. Then I closed up the car, got in, and turned the key in the ignition. I forgot to put the music on for the longest time. The amazing memory of the path of light kept playing in my mind.

For one timeless moment, I believed that I could walk on water. The memory is a kindness that was bestowed on me.

Readers Response

Jozef Imrich, Esq. said, "Being able to walk on water means to know how it feels to be poor and rich all at the same time. A friend sent this to me recently ...

Being poor is knowing exactly how much everything costs

Being poor is getting angry at your kids for asking for all the crap they see on TV.

Being poor is having to keep buying $800 cars because they're what you can afford, and then having the cars break down on you, because there's not an $800 car in America that's worth a dam.

Being poor is hoping the toothache goes away.

Being poor is knowing your kid goes to friends' houses but never has friends over to yours.

Being poor is going to the restroom before you get in the school lunch line so your friends will be ahead of you and won't hear you say "I get free lunch" when you get to the cashier.

Being poor is living next to the freeway.

Being poor is coming back to the car with your children in the back seat, clutching that box of Raisin Bran you just bought and trying to think of a way to make the kids understand that the box has to last.

Being poor is wondering if your well-off sibling is lying when he says he doesn't mind when you ask for help.

Being poor is off-brand toys.

Being poor is a heater in only one room of the house.

Being poor is knowing you can't leave $5 on the coffee table when your friends are around.

Being poor is hoping your kids don't have a growth spurt.

Being poor is stealing meat from the store, frying it up before your mom gets home and then telling her she doesn't have to make dinner tonight because you're not hungry anyway.

Being poor is Goodwill underwear.

Being poor is not enough space for everyone who lives with you.

Being poor is feeling the glued soles tear off your supermarket shoes when you run around the playground.

Being poor is your kid's school being the one with the 15-year-old textbooks and no air conditioning.

Being poor is thinking $8 an hour is a really good deal.

Being poor is relying on people who don't give a damn about you.

Being poor is an overnight shift under florescent lights.

Being poor is finding the letter your mom wrote to your dad, begging him for the child support.

Being poor is a bathtub you have to empty into the toilet.

Being poor is stopping the car to take a lamp from a stranger's trash.

Being poor is making lunch for your kid when a cockroach skitters over the bread, and you looking over to see if your kid saw.

Being poor is believing a GED actually makes a goddamned difference.

Being poor is people angry at you for just walking around in the mall.

Being poor is not taking the job because you can't find someone you trust to watch your kids.

Being poor is the police busting into the apartment right next to yours.

Being poor is not talking to that girl because she'll probably just laugh at your clothes.

Being poor is hoping you'll be invited for dinner.

Being poor is a sidewalk with lots of brown glass on it.

Being poor is people thinking they know something about you by the way you talk.

Being poor is needing that 35-cent raise.

Being poor is your kid's teacher assuming you don't have any books in your home.

Being poor is six dollars short on the utility bill and no way to close the gap.

Being poor is crying when you drop the mac and cheese on the floor.

Being poor is knowing you work as hard as anyone, anywhere.

Being poor is people surprised to discover you're not actually stupid.

Being poor is people surprised to discover you're not actually lazy.

Being poor is a six-hour wait in an emergency room with a sick child asleep on your lap.

Being poor is never buying anything someone else hasn't bought first.

Being poor is picking the 10 cent ramen instead of the 12 cent ramen because that's two extra packages for every dollar.

Being poor is having to live with choices you didn't know you made when you were 14 years old.

Being poor is getting tired of people wanting you to be grateful.

Being poor is knowing you're being judged.

Being poor is a box of crayons and a $1 coloring book from a community center Santa.

Being poor is checking the coin return slot of every soda machine you go by.

Being poor is deciding that it's all right to base a relationship on shelter.

Being poor is knowing you really shouldn't spend that buck on a Lotto ticket.

Being poor is hoping the register lady will spot you the dime.

Being poor is feeling helpless when your child makes the same mistakes you did, and won't listen to you beg them against doing so.

Being poor is a cough that doesn't go away.

Being poor is making sure you don't spill on the couch, just in case you have to give it back before the lease is up.

Being poor is a $200 paycheck advance from a company that takes $250 when the paycheck comes in.

Being poor is four years of night classes for an Associates of Art degree.

Being poor is a lumpy futon bed.

Being poor is knowing where the shelter is.

Being poor is people who have never been poor wondering why you choose to be so.

Being poor is knowing how hard it is to stop being poor.

Being poor is seeing how few options you have.

Being poor is running in place.

Being poor is people wondering why you didn't leave."

ME Strauss said, "Good noring Jozef. Thank you for giving me that. It's something I needed to hear. I appreciate it. Please tell the friend who sent you that that I said thank you too."

Jozef Imrich, Esq. said, "Dear Liz, (indeed, you have a lovely name)

Only if you have been in the deepest valley can you know how magnificent it is to be on the highest mountain. ~Richard Nixon

"May you discover the highest mountains wherever you drive ... You are worth it ...

"Same friend is passing on this soulful post:

'The great lesson of Don Giovanni lies at the end of the opera. Don Giovanni has been dragged down into the inferno, but Mozart does not end the opera there. Six characters come out and sing a last sextet. what is Mozart saying? He is saying, life goes on. It is probably the most profound thing anyone can say. as one of Beckett's characters says, I can't go on. I'll go on.

"Nixon said it too. Everything came to end for him, or seemed to, but he too discovered, life goes on. you start to hear the birds again, the sunshine starts to warm you again, the light starts to come back again. I know it's easy for someone else to say, but I always think, if life went on for people who went through concentration camps and lost all their families, why should it not for the rest of us.'"

ME Strauss said, "Jozef, you have that wisdom already. I know you do. I have gained that learning myself . . . that is how I can be such a Pollyanna. Hope. Your friend speaks of hope. That is what lets us see and keeps us walking for our hopeful eyes always have something to look forward to, and that looking heals our hearts and mends our souls."

Jozef Imrich, Esq. said, "Indeed, sunny Liz. As the Slavic saying notes - hope dies last."

ME Strauss said, "Jozef, I had not heard that, but I sure like it. Thanks for sharing it. Hope dies last."

Garnet said, "Liz- I am learning about you, slowly. Blogging makes it a little harder, and in some ways easier. (I've been thinking about this after Ned's most recent poem, "blogging poetry")

"I'm sorry the world weighed on you. You are strong, but you are also incredibly sensitive, and that makes the weight heavier still. I'm glad you found a way to heal yourself. Usually we know best how to heal ourselves, though it's nice when friends can help. Sharing this beautiful story, beautifully written, helps me remember to listen to my own healing voice. Recently, I've stopped living much, because I'm blogging so much. This is not your concern, but your story tells me I have to stay balanced.

"Walking on Water. You come as close as anyone I've ever known. Love, David"

ME Strauss said, "David, what a beautiful comment and compliment to my story, to me, and to you for writing it. What words could thank you adequately this writer doesn't know. Many would say you've done the impossible by setting me speechless.

"I assure you I don't walk on water. But it was nice for a second to believe that I could. The tears in my eyes are love and gratitude for a very dear friend."

Trée said, "Liz, I can't find my own words to say thanks so an unknown author is standing in for me today.

A hundred hearts would be too few
To carry all my love for you.

"I trust you understand "love" in the context of gratitude and thoughtfulness. I would really like to say more to express my gratitude but since I'm in a quoting mood today, I'll finish with Stephen King of all people:

The most important things are the hardest to say, because words diminish them.

"My arms are heavy again, but it's a good heavy. Thank you Liz and may peace be with you also."

ME Strauss said, "Hello, Tree. Thank you for coming by to read about peace as I told you I would write about it.

"Thank you too for such lovely gifts of words you send my way. I'm smiling with them."

dog1net said, "Something I've started to notice about your writing lately is that you're taking chances to really reach out and connect by asking the ever-imposing larger question and then searching for its answer wherever it may find you. "Walking on Water," is satisfying on many levels. The need to get away, to just go, to put the demands of the day behind you, but without knowing necessarily where you're going, to let yourself be in the moment, and let the car take you along until you stopped at Nick's Diner.

"Your careful description of what you ate, and the interaction you had with Doris really concretized that very human need to be connected in all things no matter what, yet at the same time to pull back and take a breather. From there, though, is where your essay really starts to explore that existential aspect of life that has all of us throwing our hands up in the air sometimes. That nasty sometimes-overpowering question of "Who am I?" And though we may not necessarily discover a direct answer, we do find it indirectly by the things we find ourselves attuned with by observing and describing what's in front of us, by the peaceful environment we have allowed ourselves to become enveloped by.

"It is there that you discover and realize that "the magic of a sunset can cure an aching heart, can still a restless mind." And there you stay "until the path of light had faded into the water." Beautiful, Liz. Just absolutely beautiful. I am walking on water with you. ~Scot"

ME Strauss said, "Thank you Scot, for naming what it is that is changing about what I'm doing. I feel a pull, but don't know where it's going. I fear that I'm disappointing some . . . I still have plenty of other stories for them.

"I appreciate especially how you've taken time to explain this one to me. It is different from the rest. I've never been so draw to detail before, but here the details demanded to be part. I had to make them real. This could not be some flight of fantasy it had to be an actual experience. Maybe that is the difference.

"Your comment is what got me to think that through, to verbalize that difference. Thank you, Scot. I'm proud to have you walk with me. ~Liz"

Mellissa said, "Elegantly written. I just took the most beautiful trip with you - in my mind's eye."

ME Strauss said, "Hello, Melissa. Welcome, You're new around here. Come in and tell us about you.

"Thank you for your lovely compliment about my writing. It's nice that you could see what I could see."

Mark Daniels said, "Changes in routine, especially to take time in God's natural world, has a way of restoring me when I feel burdened. That was true for my wife and me when we took a walk on a nature trail that runs along the Little Miami River today.

"Liz, this is a wonderful piece of writing and a great reflection on the need to get away so that we can enter the demanding places of life with confidence, hope, and joy. That whole Sabbath thing makes sense, I guess. Thanks for calling this piece to my attention."

ME Strauss said, "Hello, Mark. Yes, being out in creation makes it easier to say yes to the invitation. Thanks for sharing with me tonight as well. I left my comments on your site."

Liz said, "You know, I used to take long bus rides around this island I live on whenever I feel stressed out. I think maybe I should do that again, take a long bus ride to nowhere, or maybe to the beach or my favorite park and just sit alone and enjoy the surroundings. I haven't done that for a long time come to think of it."

Kelley Bell said, "ahha, syncronicity.

"I wanted to ask everyone, What do you want from me? I can't walk on water."

LOL And over on my bloggy, I just posted a thing about atoms. They are not solid. Just energy and empty space.

So what is holding us all in place? What is solid?

If a chair is just atoms, which are just energy and empty space, like water, then why can one hold us while the other can not?

Quantum Physics teaches that energy is not a thing, but rather, just the probability of ideas.

Therefore, Ideas Create Reality.

And if all this is true, then why is it so unthinkable that someone who BELIEVES she can walk on water [and] actually can."

ME Strauss said, "Hi, Liz. What a wonderful idea. The one time I was on Singapore was for a short one night, but I saw enough to have an idea of what that might be like. I also remember thinking when I saw the bowling alley tucked away (like everything) on the beautiful road coming in from the airport that one day I wanted to bring my friends their so that we could all say that we'd been to Singapore and gone bowling."

ME Strauss said, "Oh Kelley, I am laughing. Yes it is for a reason. What you wrote in my "Walk on Water" Post.

Quantum Physics teaches that energy is not a thing, but rather, just the probability of ideas.

Therefore, Ideas Create Reality. And if all this is true, then why is it so unthinkable that someone who BELIEVES she can walk on water actually can.

"It is not that what you say is wise. Wisdom is not such a hard thing to come by, I don't think. There is much intelligence and wisdom all around us. People just don't listen for it.

"It is that you have such a beautiful, musical, truly elegant sense of joyful humor about how you share things. Thank you, thank you, thank you."

Liz said, "Beautiful road coming in from the airport that one day I wanted to bring my friends their so that we could all say that we'd been to Singapore and gone bowling.

"hehe...well, if you ever come this way again, let me know. And if you want to bowl, I'm game."

ME Strauss said, "Hi, Liz. One never knows. That was a past life, but this could be a past life too someday.

"That sure would be fun--a great book title too: "Bowling in Singapore""

Kelley Bell said, "I am laughing too."

ME Strauss said, "YEA! Kelley. Then we laugh together."

Eric Mutta said, "Poetic as always. It's your writing signature."

ME Strauss said, "Hi, Eric. Thank you. I'm glad you liked it."

Social Conformity

A while back I was sitting in the neighborhood bar talking to a professor of psychology. I was asking him about the people who work for me.

"I don't understand," I said. "He walked into my office and told me it was the best of it's kind that he'd ever worked on. He was proud of it. I thought I had finally gotten him to think. He was certainly seeing what the payoff is. But the next time around he was back to underachieving again."

My friend, the professor took out his pen, pulled over a napkin, and began to explain the Asch test to me. I was both interested and invested. I sipped my wine and listened attentively.

"Dr. Asch sat a group of people around a table. All but one were confederates in the experiment. Asch showed them two cards, like these two. He asked them each to say which line on the second was the same length as that on the first. All but one answered the question before it was the subject's turn. All chose the obviously wrong choice, say for example, the too long third one. Then Dr. Asch turned to the subject and asked for an answer. Put on the spot in a group, 34% of the subjects gave the group answer consistently even when the experiment was repeated, and 74% agreed with the group at least once. "

Now I was floored. Talk about speechless.

"But the answer is obvious." I said setting my wine on the bar, leaning in, looking for some explanation.

"Yes, that's the point," he said. "Still most people choose to go with the group. They don't want to look silly or take a risk. You can take heart that it changes if one other person chooses the right answer, if the subject sees some support."

"If someone else will be brave," I said without feeling.

"That's one explanation."

I was shaking my head and looking at my hands long before the next words came out.

"I couldn't do that," I said. "It would physically hurt me." I looked up from the lines on the napkin, a pained expression that I could feel on my face. "I would hate it, but I would have to say no. What use would I be to anyone, if I didn't say what I see? The whole thing doesn't make sense to me. . . . I believe it—I've lived it—but I don't understand it."

"It's called social conformity."

Dr. Asch was still working on why it happens. When he died he wasn't sure whether some subjects hadn't convinced themselves the group answer was correct. Kind of explains how two reporters can cover the same event and write up two entirely different stories.

My dad used to say "Don't believe anything you hear and only half of what you see."

He said a lot about honesty, but not a word about conformity.

Readers Response

Mark Cross said, "As I mentioned in a comment on my site today. We learn this behavior in grade school and carry it into our adult lives. I call it pack mentality but social conformity works too."

ME Strauss said, "Mark! Yeah, I think we grown-ups have it worse than the kids."

Mark Cross said, "Very much so. You see it all around you. At work, in social gathers, inter-personal relationships and natural disasters."

ME Strauss said, "My thoughts exactly."

garnet said, "People must think there's some trick, a double meaning to the test, or the question. Yes, pack mentality snags us daily. I am pretty contrarian in my choices: almost no TV, few magazines, less consumerist, less aggressive about goals, into the present. But I often feel palpable social exclusion by the majority. As I mature, and through blogging, I've started to find others who orbit as far out as me."

iamnasra said, "Loved this article...it shows how the mind works..."

ME Strauss said, "Garnet, it's good to realize as we get older that the universe has many who aren't like the rest--sort of a minority majority. I've found that people who write tend to be that way by nature. smiles, Liz"

ME Strauss said, "Lamnasra, thank you. I've been thinking about this for a while now. The way the mind works is interesting to me as well. smiles, Liz"

Jennifer said, "When I was younger, I would have rather died than stand out from the group. Now that I am older, I find myself wanting to be unique and different from everyone else.

"Yet if a group chose an obviously wrong answer, I would start to doubt myself. I would think the group saw something I was missing. I think it boils down to self-confidence more than conformity. But being only one person, I am not a representative sample of the population."

ME Strauss said, "Jennifer, thank you for explaining it in a way that makes sense to me. THAT I can understand. Not being sure that you're missing something is something I'm always wondering about. I think most of the time I am. smiles, Liz"

Lee Carlon said, "It is interesting, and I think it would be people with a little more confidence in themselves that give the answer they believe is correct.

"I'm fairly used to going a different way to most people, not so much because I want to stand out, but because I know what I want/think and rarely change that just to conform with other people. Good post, Liz."

Ned said, "I am used to never having the same answer or opinion as anyone, let alone the group. I fear it may just be the fact that I am contrary rather than any individualism that I am exhibiting... sigh. It does seem to hold true that people are more comfortable with their opinions if others will agree and support them. It is part of human nature to want to be an individual, but not part of our nature to want to feel isolated. I suppose it is all a delicate dance between a need to be different and a need to be accepted."

ME Strauss said, "Thanks for your thoughts, Lee. I too am used to being the odd man out. It would be hard for me to think that people just weren't seeing what was there. I would literally be moving in my seat. smiles, Liz"

ME Strauss said, "Ned, you make such a good point. We want to be individual yet part of the group. It seems that people will give up their individuality to stay part of the group they don't know. I guess that when we're used to not having the same answer as the group, we learn to find value in why that is so. Your right it is a delicate balance, though. smiles, Liz"

rhein said, "*"the way the mind works..."* Didn't someone say there is 3 frontiers left to humanity- the depths of the sea, the depths of space, and the depths of the human mind? I've been trying to figure out how to add a link on my site to the photographer story you wrote."

ME Strauss said, "Rhein, you are right about those three frontiers. Though with some of us, I suspect we might qualify for individual numbers on own. You know, frontier numbers 4, 5, 6, etc. I'll get the link info and bring it over. smiles, Liz"

melly said, "When I was a teenager and a youth group guide I used to start my session on Nazi Germany with this same test. I'd ask one of the kids to leave, explain the test to the group, and then call the kid back inside the room. I did that because one of the most prevalent questions when talking to kids about what happened back then is - but how come no one said anything or stood up?

"Every once in a while a kid surprised me and stood his/ her ground. You could never tell who these non-conforming kids would be in advance. Sometimes the popular ones, sometimes the nerdy/smart ones, and sometimes the annoying ones. It remained a mystery."

ME Strauss said, "Melly, what a great story. I had you been on the other end one of those kids would have been you. smiles, me-Liz

Anonymous (E) said, "Hello Crayon Lady! Ever heard of Zimbardo's Prison Experiment? I disagree w/ned in that it seems much more a trait of human nature to want & feel like one belongs to the group, is accepted as part of it.

"All sorts of survival value in that behavior - and then there are the "misfits". Healthy societies tolerate them (just in case conditions change & that sort of behavior has advantages,) but by & large, organizations/societies prefer conformists."

ME Strauss said, "Hi, Anonymous E! No I've not heard of Zimbardo's Prison Experiment, but I hear you suggesting that I find out about it.

"You are a wise man to agree with Ned, she knows many things and quotes both Popeye and Kipling. But doesn't society need misfits for conformists to frown upon? smiles, Liz"

Anonymous (E) said, "'But doesn't society need misfits for conformists to frown upon?'

"No. Generalizing, the 'misfits' are usually the creative types who help to move a society in different, new, directions. Conformists will always predominate but a healthy society will allow & maintain a certain amount of diversity.

"Just be thankful you don't live at a time when the Inquisition is busy - but then again, isn't there always some form of Inquisition at work?"

ME Strauss said, "Ah Anonymous E! The misfits have to strive for a balance between diversification and integration. The conformists determine the key and the price to the latter, possibly asking the misfits to choose between fitting in and sanity.

"You're right there is always an inquisition of some sort--usually perpetrated by a mind that carries some sort of ego insecurity. smiles, Liz"

Anonymous said, "You once mentioned that Australians think very differently re categorization?

"Isn't it true that, in general, societies have different tolerances for non-conformists? It's part of what differentiates one from another - I'm thinking here of Japan, where, seems to me, there is a much, much higher value for conformity than here in the U.S.

"All in all, I think we're incredibly lucky to be living in this place, at this time. Creativity, individuality, independence is valued much higher here than it is in other places around the world. Just a thought..."

ME Strauss said, "Anon E: Funny you should mention that I was just reading today that in Japan in certain situations, kids are called up to be nonconformists. They all do so in the same way. The Japanese person writing was bemoaning the fact that they were conforming in their nonconformity.

"I do feel lucky to be in this country at this time and am delighted to hear you shout such good news. We misfits need to understand that this isn't such a bad place to be. smiles, Liz"

Garnet said, "Some thoughts after reading all these rich comments. Conformity can also be good, a positive influence.

It can break people out of weak habits by pressuring then to straighten up.

"And non-conformists, outsiders, may grow stronger by that exclusion, may develop greater compassion through the pain and loneliness. They are more willing to tell the truth as they see it.

"In some ancient societies, the outsiders were seen as shamans, like the idiot savant, or the berdashe. Some societies reap the benefits and some do not. This difference could be seen as a barometer of a society's health."

Zephan said, "Social conformity is for the birds!!! And this is coming from a fifteen year-old. I'm a sophomore, and while all my peers are busy nattering on and on about who they're going out with, or what they should wear, I just stand there, rolling my eyes. I'm a loner, I don't care much for people, and I loathe all of those incompetent, oafish cads who think they have to act like everyone else and worry about it 24/7. I mean, Come on, people! Get some lives! Okay, I'm done ranting...I just need some info. for my speech topic."

ME Strauss said, "Good for you, zephan. I'm with you 100%, which why I chose this topic to write about. smiles, Liz"

Mark McGrath

Tyke Johnson

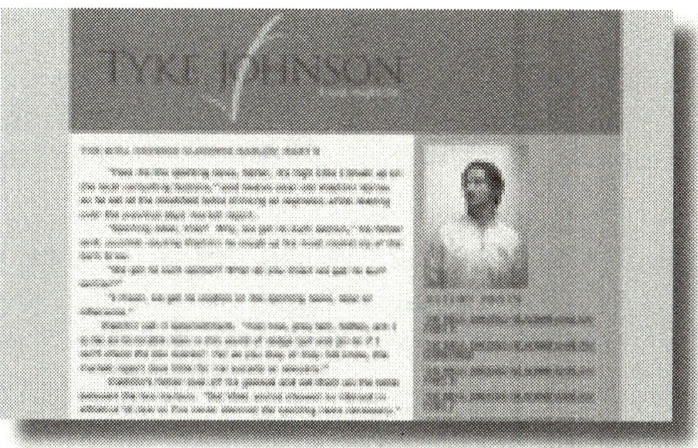

My name is Mark McGrath. I live in a place called Los Angeles, where many names are pronounced wrong.

The Well-Dressed Vladimir Karlov: Part 8

"Do not spill a drop of that or I shall sell you to the gypsies," twelve-year-old Vladimir Karlov threatened. His mother was anxiously hanging over a pot of boiling soup, trying to pour some into a platinum thermos. "I spent three hours last night making that delicacy you're fumbling with and I'll not have a fool-handed mistress of the night ruin it for me."

On any other day Vladimir would have held his tongue, for he was a firm believer in the classical household hierarchy. However, any other day was not the first day of school.

The year prior was a fretful one, a mixture of benign teachers holding hands with benign children. Circles and squares on chalkboards. Backwards mathematics. Unintelligible cursive with oversized loops and heart-shaped dots.

When asked the answer to a simple geometric equation, a girl named Elissa mentioned that her favorite color was blue. When a boy named Tyler was asked the same question he began talking about soccer and pepperoni pizza. Then the old bag turned to Vlad.

"Can you help us out, Vlad?"

"I cannot, simpleton? For you and your union of dim-witted hags are beyond help. I'll not learn about asymmetrical circles and slanted squares that adorn a beaten chalkboard and fill these scraps you call books. Did they not teach you of a compass in your club, old lady? Has there been no mention of rulers? No, gray-haired governess, I'll not say a thing, I'll not say a word."

"It seems you already have. And quite a lot at that." She smiled at her wit and the kids shared in it, with echoing laughter that filled the classroom. Vladimir stood atop his desk and puffed out his chest, pointing his fingers to the peons below.

"Laugh it up, trolls. Laugh till you wet yourselves and forget the name on your book bags. You bore me with your stories of circular cheese and longhaired dolls. Your stained paints and knotted hair. Your colorful lunch pails and individual servings of pudding. Are you aware of what you're eating, you buffoons? Are you aware of anything at all!?"

Vladimir walked east, soup in tow, thinking about the year before. At least the old bag is gone he thought, "at least the old bag is gone."

The school was a massive wall of cracking red. Brick with granite in between. As Vladimir approached the building, he assumed a conversation with the graying security guard. "How dare they allow, let alone expect, children to enter the confines of this looming disaster."

"Seems they think it's best for you, Vlad. Keeps you off the streets I guess."

"Seems the district has spent too much money on prostituting our local squares for giant monuments of pointy scrap metal in honor of some hack who's decided his adolescent doodling is high art."

"Seems you don't like school, Vlad."

"Seems you might just want to turn your back when I sneak out this very gate after homeroom."

"Seems you might just get stopped, Vlad."

Vladimir realized his scheme to disappear before the brunt of first period and the dragging day to follow had a minor fault.

"You're a tall man, Sir and I barely reach your waist. Surely you wouldn't notice such a small one passing by."

"I may be tall, Vlad, but I'm always looking down."

"Then look down no more, Gray Beard, for I'll not fraternize with a communist another moment. Your shirt and pants may be blue and black, but your eyes and tongue are red."

Vladimir stomps off, as the security guard stares no higher than his waist.

Inside, the halls reek of linoleum and bleach and the yelling of his classmates resound off the "Welcome Back" walls. He walks with disdain for the posters, knowing they'll be gone by the following week, when the teacher's joy of being back will have dissipated as much as their students' had.

Vladimir carries his thermos tight to his body, walking as close to the Crayola propaganda as he can. The hall rushes with blond-haired boys and red-haired girls and in Vladimir's experience, blond-haired boys and red-haired girls were never one for manners.

At the age of eleven, while Vladimir was walking through the woods in search of a Huron Indian burial ground, he happened upon first year teens Maura Finnegan and Kyle Kolemann. Maura was a freckled-faced redhead with an obsession for green whose parents must have convinced her the adage "all red heads look good in green" was true, for she went wild on the idea, and though Vladimir would usually agree with this statement, Maura was the unfortunate exception. Her freckles and pale skin were so obviously green in their heritage that the Kelly addition made it hard to look at her, let alone do what Kyle Kolemann, the blond-haired soccer player was doing. It seems his Nazi poster child heritage meshed so well with the smell of wet potatoes that neither of them could resist each other any longer and they had no choice but to fall down and grope one another's non-gropable sexual parts right where the Huron's were once laid to rest.

Vladimir noticed that Maura's shirt and training bra had been strewn atop a group of stones that could have once covered the body of a Huron child, but seeing as Vladimir was all of a sudden quite aroused by the scene that was unfolding before his eyes, he couldn't help but hold back his emotions at the outrage of the historical raping. Still he thought, to make sure no bones were being trampled upon, "I should go in for a closer look."

At his feet, scattered amongst the dirt were ancient arrowheads and a pair of boys' Fruit of the Looms. They were white and small, like a childish cartoon character, and Vladimir couldn't get over it. While the two drunken nations continued their abomination of childhood innocence, Vladimir stared at the small white underwear, fearing that perhaps his own Fruit of the Looms looked just as small when lying around his room. Or was it the dirt and stone environment that made them look so small? An overwhelming fear rushed over Vladimir and before he could stop himself, he grabbed for the underwear and turned to make a break for it. However, his luck proved to be as bad as his coordination, and he fell over himself, landing amongst the pile of sin.

Vladimir, underwear in hand, went on the offensive before the two could say a word.

"This is a place of worship and remembrance, not of debauchery and sin."

"A place of heroes and courage, not of weak will and faint heart."

"Of honor and contemplation, not of fast hands and skinny thighs, petite breasts and wet navels, arched backs and long necks, pubic hair and –"

The Huron burial ground was a soft bed and when Vladimir came to, he had one black eye and a welt on the back of his head from the tombstone he had chose for a pillow. He stood up slowly and tried to shake off the dirt that was embedded into his hair and twill jacket, but his head hurt too much for the shaking. Then, after confirmation of all working parts, he searched for a small piece of cotton. Five minutes later he quit, nothing had been left behind. The selfish voyeurs had taken everything they brought, not leaving a single thing for their guest; something he learned in Victorian Manner's Class was the first sign that a person had no manners.

Homeroom was a raging affair. Kids on their desks and paper flying in all directions. Several misguided paper airplanes hit Vladimir and with each offense his threats to the engineers got worse.

"Nikkos you Grecian sloth, as if your weight and smell weren't offensive enough, now you've taken to aeronautical paper mischief. Hit me again with one of your devilish contraptions and I'll see to it that your parents and siblings don't see the outside of a South African gold mine as long as they live."

Moments later another hit Vladimir on the cheek.

"David, you fop of a king's man. I'll not be attacked by such a weak-minded zealot. Hold your tongue and hand, you prince of karaoke law and dance hall scripture, or I shall steal your father's hats and robes and sell them back to the dandies in the boys' district where they belong."

Both David and Nikkos teamed up and began to approach Vladimir for a more intimate offensive, but a striking Italian woman with full brown hair, half pulled into a ponytail, came bursting into the room, delaying the boys' angry steps.

She wore a clay-colored blouse and flowing black skirt and she smelled as if she just came in from the vineyards. Vladimir's nostrils cleared and grapes came pouring in. He had never breathed so deep. After setting her fashionably beaten handbag on her desk, she began writing on the chalkboard with long exaggerated motions. The letters were in cursive and it took a moment for Vladimir to make it out. "The two god damnit, the two," he cursed aloud.

"That's the letter Q," she said, ignoring Vladimir's cursing, "and it all spells out Quaranta."

Quaranta, he thought, Quaranta, "it all spells out Quaranta."

"That's right, Young Sir, and what may I ask is your name?"

"Vladimir Soft Fists Karlov," Tyler yelled aloud. It seemed the pepperoni-pizza-loving misfit had somehow passed the fifth grade.

Vladimir played it cool, hoping the pacifist approach would impress his new seductress.

"My name is Vladimir Karlov, and I assure you my lady, my fists, like many parts of my body, are by no means soft."

Vladimir took Ms. Quaranta's shocked reaction as a good sign. It meant she knew all about those parts in boys' pants that went purple and red and blue when she bent over and fixed her heel or put a loose hair behind her ear. That ass could sit on the chalk board ledge, Vladimir thought, "that ass could sit on the chalk board ledge."

Though she didn't blush at either comment, Vladimir was confident that there were other pink parts on her body becoming quite flush.

The next hour was spent calling roll and assigning desks. The boys said their names and told Ms. Quaranta about soccer and football and baseball while the girls told her about purses and singers and makeup, but all Vladimir could think of was the busty Mediterranean before him.

When Vladimir was finally called on, he stood, unbuttoned his velvet suit jacket, and cleared his throat with a cough. "My name is Vladimir Karlov and I know nothing of soccer or football or baseball. I know nothing of purses or singers or makeup, but I do know how to pleasure. Yes, my Roman senior, I do know how to pleasure."

Vladimir was sure he saw some pink.

Moments later Vladimir was walking to the principle's office with a note describing his sexual comments. It was folded and placed in an envelope, which Ms. Quaranta, eyes shut, licked to seal.

"It's worth the punishment to see just that," Vladimir said, "it's worth the punishment for that."

And he was walking down the hall with her tongue on his mind and an erection tearing through his pants.

"Turns out she doesn't like compliments, turns out she's just a prude."

"Turns out you said some things here Vlad, some things one might call lewd."

Vladimir was pleading his case to Henry who was reading the note with heavy brow from behind a large oak desk. A bottle of scotch sat between them.

"I only meant to speak highly."

"Speaking highly, this is assumed?"

"And I hold her at the greatest heights."

"But this moistness is all presumed?"

Vladimir pulled his chair in closer to the desk.

"Pour me another and I'll tell you more, pour me another and I'll show you her door."

Henry poured the heavy scotch into a copper mug and Vladimir took it down in haste.

"It may be over ice but it still heats my loins."

Vladimir pushed forward the mug.

"Fill it again 'til I can't feel my loins."

As he gave himself a tug.

Henry set the note aside and looked over the desk, watching Vladimir pull down pour after pour.

"You're approaching it all wrong, Vlad."

"Of course I am. Of course."

"You're not giving her what she wants, Vlad."

"Of course, I'll go right for the source."

Vladimir stands up holding his pride in his hand.

"I shall march in and shower her with love."

"Vlad, the Italian wants more."

"I shall march in and shower her with hugs."

"Vlad, the Italian wants more."

"What can I do?" Vladimir pleads, drinking another pour down, "what can I do," on his knees, "and not be just another clown?"

"Perhaps she likes humor, Vlad, perhaps she likes all the rest."

"You mean like David and Tyler and Nikkos, my friend?"

"Perhaps she likes them the best."

"But they speak of nothing and nothing, and act all the same."

"And if you keep doing nothing and nothing, your act is all in vain."

"Henry, I acted before my walk, my walk to come see you."

"Vlad, your act was just a joke, and that's all she sees in you."

Vladimir stood up, the bottle empty and dry, desperately trying to figure out what Henry had meant this time.

His eyes raced around the room 'til they fell upon a giant golden trophy that was protected by a newly streak-free-shined pain of glass. Vladimir puffed out his chest and tightened his belt a notch.

"These walls will cave before I die, Henry they'll crash and break, but I'll have the Italian before they fall, Henry make no mistake."

Vladimir stood outside the classroom looking through the long pane of glass that extended the length of the door. The top poured out her hair, the bottom carved her calves, and the middle saw bust and butt. Her skirt swung around getting caught on her own full ass when she made any movement other than forward. Vladimir watched and waited for each turn to the board or desk, then back to the students again. He watched in agony, throbbing in loin and lip, for the scotch did nothing to cure the bursting below.

"She wants trophies, Vlad, she wants gold."

"I'll give her as many as I can."

"She wants more than you can offer, Vlad, the Italian wants a man."

Vladimir burst into the room, slamming the door to the board, while the class stared on with wide eyes, as Vladimir brandished his sword.

He then jumped atop his desk, pointing his burning youth at Ms. Quaranta who dropped the book in her hand.

"Roman temptress come handle me, come wrap me in your skirt. Roman temptress, come ravage me, no longer be just a flirt."

But Vladimir was losing his voice and his head was beginning to ache, and he looked around to find Henry as his legs began to shake. And as he hit the ground he caught a glimpse, of vineyards he once dreamed, where her thick black hair curled around his neck, and her smell was all that it seemed.

Readers Response

thick and black said, "The hair was so thick. so black. Rubbed up against my crotch. Brutal and menacing, like rape in the afternoon, it awoke me."

James said, "Dude that is so sick and twisted. Your a sick pervert. You need to be in a 6 by 6 room for the rest of your life. You really need Jesus man."

MaryAnn McNeil
Writer's Blog

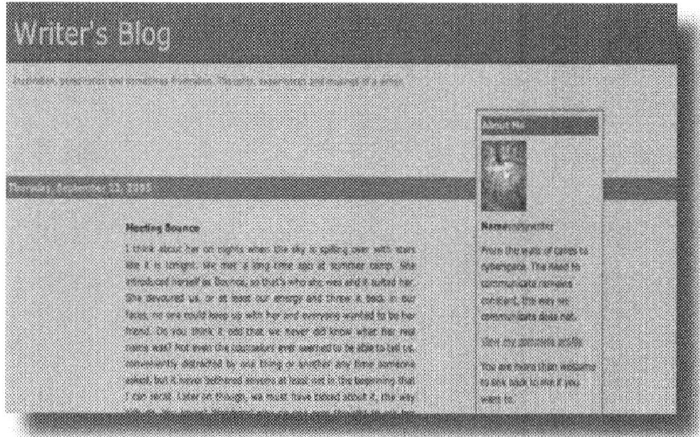

Mary Ann McNeil blogs under the handle easywriter at Writer's Blog. This was a two part post that garnered favorable response with my readers and is a piece attention among my readers.

Meeting Bounce

I think about her on nights when the sky is spilling over with stars like it is tonight. We met a long time ago at summer camp. She introduced herself as Bounce, so that's who she was and it suited her. She devoured us, or at least our energy and threw it back in our faces, no one could keep up with her and everyone wanted to be her friend. Do you think it odd that we never did know what her real name was? Not even the counselors ever seemed to be able to tell us, conveniently distracted by one thing or another any time someone asked, but it never bothered anyone at least not in the beginning that I can recall. Later on though, we must have talked about it, the way kids do. You know? Wondered why no one ever thought to ask her themselves. Why didn't we? Strange.

When we reminisce about her now, and that doesn't happen often, it's as if she is frozen in time. Caught in a snippet of film that begins with one innocent eleven year old's question and ends in a drawn out, breathless silence. Just that one night, that one conversation, playing itself out endlessly in our memories. It's as if all other traces of her existence in our lives during those three weeks ended up on the cutting room floor.

Clear as day, I can see her sitting cross-legged on the ground outside our tent, holding the flashlight up to her chin, asking us if she looked different from the rest of us and you know what? She did. Her eyes were great pools of black in a too pale face. Her hair a luminescent white halo around her head. In the stark light and shadows playing over her face she transcended the eerie look the rest of us had when we, each of us, took the lamp in our turn and tried it for ourselves. I think that the first time we ever admitted something wasn't right. But it wasn't just the look of her, it was her voice too, it added new depths to our unease.

Oh, if you could have heard her voice as she spun her tale, unearthly, drifting, dreamy, catching us in its spell and dragging us into her peculiar reality holding us too quiet until long after she finished. Well, we didn't know what to think, what to say when she was done. We laughed mostly, but not then, not right away; we waited until the morning, we teased her without mercy, avoided her. Dear God we were cruel, but you have to understand. It was fear that drove us. A terror that built itself up in our minds. Something alien had entered our midst and we were afraid that in spite of the outlandishness of her claim, it could be true. Yeah, I suppose anything is possible, after all, it looks as though Mars was vibrant and alive at one time.

What Bounce Said

After Bounce made us wake up and notice that she didn't really look quite the same as the rest of us and after we all sat staring at her with our mouths hanging open for a while she seemed to slide away from us. Her eyes took on a distant stare, she was looking past us, not at us and then, she started to speak. She wasn't with us anymore.

"It doesn't matter anyways whether or not I tell you, 'cause even if you said anything no one would believe you. I don't belong here, not one of you. I know it and so do you. Mom and Dad made me come, they said it would give me a chance to learn how to get along, but it's too hard. I'm tired... You all make me tired...Wanna know where I'm from?"

We all nodded in unison, entranced by her sudden transformation. Our friend Bounce was gone, a stranger had taken her place. The flashlight lay forgotten on the grass beside me, somehow we knew, the game we were playing was over. Whatever it was that was happening now was far more surreal than ghost stories or flashlights held under our chins would ever be.

"The Old Ones knew what was happening. Our world was changing...The rivers that ran as red as the sky were drying up. Animals were becoming scarce, the hunters were having to go further and further from the villages to find food. Crops had diseases that no one recognized. The winds brought sickness. Little by little everything was turning to dust.

The people from the cities had no answers, but we did because we kept close to our Old Ones and they told us. We had to find a way to leave because our home was dying, so we did that. We left our villages, moved into the cities, went to schools and learned. We were artists, story tellers, seers, healers. We loved music, cherished our ancestors and our history. We remained the keepers of our customs and traditions. But what we became...We became the scientists, technicians and pilots. There was time, just enough time and we used it well. Then, when everything was ready..."

The silence as she trailed away was deafening. I don't think any of us really knew exactly what she was saying. It all seemed too far above us, understanding hanging over our heads just a little out of reach. I tried breaking the spell, tried to get her attention.

"Bounce?" She looked at me, coming back to us, at least a little. "You haven't told us anything, just some old story you made up, it sounds like you're reading from some stupid book." She stared at me and I stared back, challenging her until I found my self drowning in her too black eyes. She let me go then, sensing my panic I suppose, or maybe just losing interest. I wasn't enough to stop her.

"I was born just before we arrived here. Someday, Mom promised me and Dad too, we're going to find a way to go back... Some day..." She was gone again so, we waited, it's not like there was anything else to do.

"I only know about it from them, they tell me the stories, what it was like. How beautiful it was...Even the cities were beautiful. That's what the people who lived there did. They built things, they made things. Wonderful things. They bought and they sold...They sold our world in the end, to the Gods of destruction."

I swear she shimmered, left our sight for an instant. Then returned, far paler than she already looked and thinner? No, elongated. Body, arms, hands and feet, long, and thin. She was too tall for a child of eleven. But it was so fleeting...

Bounce settled back into her familiar form and turned her face up to take in the night sky. "See, up there? That is where I belong. Not here. Not here. Not here.

Readers Response

Lisa said, "Breathtaking! I can see her there, in the dark."

easywriter said, "Thanks Lisa."

Carolyn said, "What I want to know is the tale she told you!"

easywriter said, "Carolyn *Pounce* I'm thinking about it!"

Melly said, "It seems that I always agree with Carolyn lately. Going to read it next. Good thing I did it in order."

easywriter said, "Oh, I guess I should have posted it backwards. Never thought of that. Oops!"

S.L. Cunningham
Unburned Pieces of the Mind

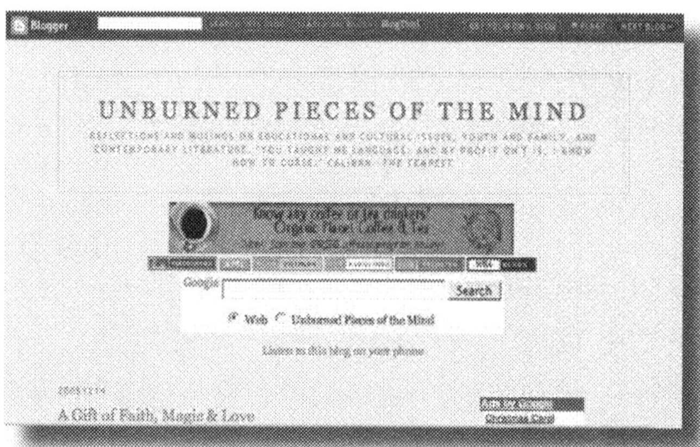

S. L. Cunningham is a freelance writer and has poems and feature articles published in several small press magazines and newspapers. A graduate of Wichita State University, he holds an MFA in English/Creative Writing and has worked the last several years as an educator and social services worker. Presently he works as an adolescent counselor for at-risk youth.

As the Shades of Evening Draw On

October is not a month that I usually associate with rain, at least not in the same sense as I do April and May, but with close to eleven inches of rain so far this month, and another two to four inches of rain expected from the storm that is raging outside, I think a long dry spell for November would be welcomed. Maybe even through December considering that here in Maine our rainfall is already twelve inches above average. However, considering the recent weather pattern we seem to be in, I imagine it won't be too long before I'm looking at snow piled right up to my windowsill.

The lights have been flickering on and off for the last half hour now. I decide it might be best to unplug the computer and TV, and just make an evening of it at my kitchen table, reading and writing in my journal. Nor'easters are always impressive, and this one so far has been putting on an incredible display of wind and rain since mid-afternoon. The trees bend in a frenzied dance, shedding leaves and small branches that scatter about in the yard and street. Bobbing like a bobble head toy, my cat puts on an amusing show of concern as it looks out the window.

The coffee maker makes its last gurgle just before the power goes out shortly. The power comes back on but it isn't too long before the lights start to flicker again. I decide enough is enough. If I'm going to have flicker, than I'll take it in the soft form of lit candles, rather than a harsh, sputtering light bulb. I get a couple of candles out and set them up on the table. Once lit, I cut the lights.

I sit down in the chair and marvel at the change of atmosphere I've created. The ambiance from the warm hue of the candles, along with the rain beating against the windows, makes me feel as if I've been transported back in time. Considering this is the week ending with Halloween, I decide what better night than this to become reacquainted with Edgar Allan Poe.

"The Fall of the House of Usher" has always been a particular favorite of mine. The opening lines especially have a sonorous, mystical quality:

During the whole of a dull, dark, and soundless day in the autumn of the year, when the clouds hung oppressively low in the heavens, had been passing alone, on horseback, through a singularly dreary tract of country; and at length found myself, as the shades of the evening drew on, within view of the melancholy House of Usher.

To read Poe is to read the wrangling of the human soul when it is no longer capable of balancing its connection with the natural world with the spiritual, when it becomes mired in its physical existence, when it becomes relegated to the "unredeemed dreariness of thought."

Holding to that sentiment I find myself drifting off into the push and pull of the wind against the building: the rain, heavy and certain. And then I wonder how it is that I sit here at this table laden with thoughts of the events that have transpired since 9/11. Something has happened to us since the collapse of the World Trade Center, something insidious and malignant has affected all of us, has changed us, whether we realize it or not, in ways that, though, may not be easily understood, is becoming more evident each day. Al Qaeda has turned our country into a "mansion of gloom." Instead of a culture of hope and optimism, we have become a culture of fear. And as such, we have become clumsy and ineffective in our response to this war of terror that has been unleashed on us.

Out of fear, we give up our liberties, our freedoms, and our privacy so that we may be protected from those who wish to do us harm. But I don't feel any safer. When I flew out to California last year, and was subjected to a full search not only of my belongings, but a pat-search as well, I did not feel like I was being protected from ruthless hijackers intent on using my flight as a bomb. As a TSA agent swept me with his wand, I couldn't rationalize how this end justified any means. Instead, I thought it terribly reminiscent of Orwell's 1984. Putting my shoes back on, I felt relieved that Big Brother determined I wasn't a threat, but, nevertheless, as far as I was concerned, the unthinkable had become reality. Our behaviors in society today are being closely monitored, and as long as terrorists wage their psychological and explosive warfare against us, I imagine it won't be very long before our very thoughts are being closely censored to protect us from Al-Qaeda's mission of merciless insanity. I pick back up where I left off on my reading and find a passage that seems almost transpicuous of our present dilemma:

"I shall perish," said he, "I must perish in this deplorable folly. Thus, thus, and not otherwise, shall I be lost. I dread the events of the future, not in themselves, but in their results. I shudder at the thought of any, even the most trivial, incident, which may operate upon this intolerable agitation of soul. I have, indeed, no abhorrence of danger, except in its absolute effect --in terror. In this unnerved-in this pitiable condition --I feel that the period will sooner or later arrive when I must abandon life and reason together, in some struggle with the grim phantasm, FEAR."

We do not have to live our lives in fear. We do not have to succumb to pernicious pessimisms that dictate the tempo of our lives. Though I may not be able to change the reality of our present political and economic situation, I can change how I respond to it and thus affect a change in my reality by choosing to live my life out of courage, hope and love. As the candles I have lit burn down, I reaffirm my belief in our humanity and God, and decide that I am not going to contribute to this "collective consciousness" of Osama Bin Laden butterflies. I like my freedom, thank you very much. And so with that I pinch off the flame of the candles. My cat, nestled against Poe's collective works, watches me with what seems a curious intent. I scoop the cat up off the table and prop him up to my shoulder.

It is a cold wind that blows tonight, the howl deep and low, the voice of winter to come. Tomorrow morning the drive to work will be that of a more wintry scene, the leaves having been blown off most of the trees, the gray clouds crabbing across the sky like sailboats heading for Isleboro. I decide that to celebrate my newfound freedom, I'm going to get up an hour earlier and walk to Weaver's Bakery in downtown Belfast. At 5:30 a.m., a tray of apple spice doughnuts will have been pulled from the fryer vat. I'll order two doughnuts with a cup of coffee, and then go outside and sit on the bench near Main and High Street. When you bite into a hot doughnut like that on a thirty-degree morning, well, I think it's about as close to heaven as you can possibly get.

Readers Response

rdl said, "My mouth is watering. Sounds like you are getting the weather we just had here in Mass. Lovely post, as usual."

ME Strauss said, "You wrote this one sort of like a bell curve inverted, but the mood was never down more introspective and disillusioned. To say I am delighted that you've found the way to make your own optimism would be the epitome of Liz understatment. Don't you think? But I have to admit a sentence that has the words 30 degrees and heaven in quite that juxtaposition seems an oxymoron to me. I'm cold for you already and you won't be there for at least three hours yet as I figure it. Part of the way I keep my optimism is to delegate the worry over the very big things, such as nuclear war. I know that others are better at it and have more practice, so I leave those kinds of worries to the experts who know how to do it well. Heaven is inside us. I'm glad you found the key."

Gone Away said, "Worry must be the cheapest commodity in the universe, the way we waste huge amounts of it every day. I'm glad you found a way to get rid of yours. Beautiful essay, as ever, Scot. Dang, you can write!"

Patry Francis said, "I love the way you weave Poe's gloom into your piece, and then haul us toward the light. You're so right. Though we may find ourselves drawn to the House of Usher, we don't have to live there."

Osinachi said, "An excellent post from your domestic perspective to a universal narrative. You are a genius."

garnet said, "Scot, you always deliver the goods. There's a gentleness in you language, which hold our hands as you lead us. The storm and your mood with the candles leads so perfectly to Poe. The message is always balanced, as it was here. Liz was right this had an inverted bell curve shape. Beautiful."

Scot said, "rdl, thanks for stopping by. I think you may have gotten more rain out of this last storm than we did. Glad you enjoyed . . ."

Scot said, "Liz, your visits are always welcomed and I especially appreciate your insightful comments. I love the image of the inverted bell curve. I hadn't quite thought of the structure of this essay in quite that way, but it fits. I hope, though, you are not finding fault with me for the oxymoron. It was, afterall, a hot doughnut, and there within lies the paradox. Thank you so much for reading and sharing."

Scot said, "Clive, your compliment is appreciated. I enjoy the contemplative quality of your writing and feel in good company when you check in."

"Patry: Thank you for that. Your comments help me gauge whether I have succeeded with tying together some of the larger elements of the work."

"Osinachi, Thank for stopping by. Your compliment is appreciated."

"Garnet: Good to see you here. I appreciate that you take the time to write such reflective responses. I especially like how you find the internal connections that have the most meaning for you, and so generously share them. Thank you, Scot"

ME Strauss said, "No Scot, no fault found. If any thing maybe what I was expressing (inadequately) was a little longing. The image of you with that hot doughnut in 30 degree weather is so romantic it does call up a kind of heaven . . . but damn if that evil self-preserver in my brain didn't leave it at that. NO, it had to tell you that I would be cold and even worse it had to do it cryptically and say "it seems an oxymoron to me." Which of course you would hear as me speaking of the literary device rather than a reference to my own discomfort with the cold. (If you recall what I wrote about the changing of the seasons this might make sense to you.) I'm sorry. I'll give my self-preserving side a good talking to.

"Scot, I find your writing so uplifting and so human. I can't imagine finding anything about it I would criticize. Thanking you for your writing. You don't know how many times it has given me just what I needed at just the right moment."

Scot said, "Liz:

"'*. . .what I was expressing . . . was a little longing.*' Now that's a deeper aspect of meaning I wasn't aware of when I wrote the last sentence to my essay, but you're so right, because in essence, it recapitulates what this essay is really about, doesn't it? And so I thank you for your clarification.

"No offense taken, I was just curious as to the confusion, which now seems was never confusion to begin with. What you did was simply put your finger on a very real human emotion, and related how it felt to you. I thank you for that, and for your kind compliments of my work."

Joe said, "Scot, I get as much satisfaction out of reading your posts as I would if I had just finished a great novel (which I never have time for). They are clever, witty, and terribly satisfying. You do make a good "pick-me-up"."

Scot said, "Joe: Good to see you here. Appreciate your compliment. I'll have to come by your way and stop in for a visit."

ME Strauss said, "I suppose Scot if you were less a writer and not so good at describing heaven. Big Chesire Cat Grin."

Phil Dillon said, "Amazing. I echo what everyone else has said. You've been given a gift and a voice. Thanks for sharing them with us. I've been thinking a lot about Winston Smith and Big Brother these days, too. It seems the world is conspiring to make us believe that two plus two is five.

"Nancy and I got back from Glorietta, NMex last night with for our five requests for proposals, sample chapters, and marketing plans plans for our "books" and were wondering how we were going maintain the call the create. Upon reading your essay this morning I saw that it won't be difficult. Having companions like you, Liz, Clive is like having friends sitting with us, urging us on through the beauty of their writing.

"While we were in Glorietta I shared with Nancy that I believe that I needed kindred spirits after all the dormant years (30 years since graduating from college). For me this is like having creative consultants searching my house for the stories and the language I want to convey them in. The stuff that's been hidden away is being found. Reading the words and stories of friends like you is, I think, a way of hearing them say, "Here they are, Phil. I found them in a hall closet.""

Scot said, "Phil: You're welcome, and I thank you for that. Good to hear your trip went well. I like the analogy of "creative consultants searching my house. . ."

"When I first started my blog, I never imagined that I would find such wonderful friends as I have in you, Liz, Clive and many others. And as "kindred spirits," I think we do inspire each other to put forth our very best. To create is one thing, but to be inspired to create is an entirely different thing."

Andrea Paulsen
Nedful Things

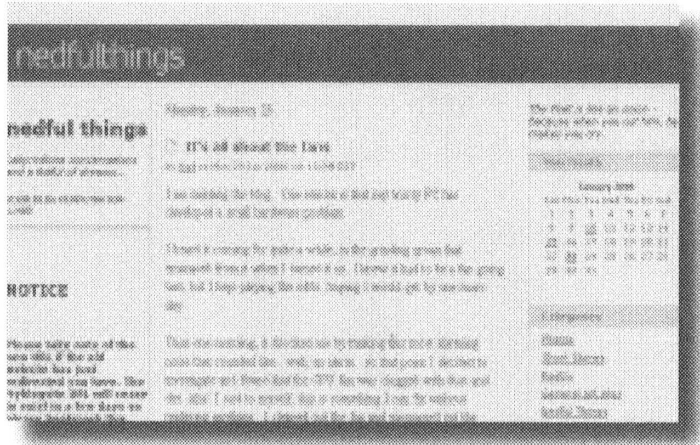

On the day I was to be born, my grandfather expired of a heart attack whilst setting up my nursery. Out of shame and guilt I declined to come forth from the womb for three more weeks, causing my mother distress and showing the reluctance towards life that would characterize my entire existence thenceforth. I reside approximately two miles away from my childhood home. I once moved as far as 9 miles away but had to return due to culture shock. It would not be inaccurate to say I resist change and the need for adaptation. Currently, I am divorced with two children, ages 6 and 11. They provide much fodder for writing themes and in return, I provide unskilled parenting. I fritter away my days on employment and income-earning, reserving the darker hours for writing. Everything else is in my poetry.

The Coffee Chronicles

Amy pulled the car into the drive-thru line which at this time of morning extended out to the street. She had made sure to leave early and the traffic was light, she would have time. As long as she got there by 8:00 she would find parking and court didn't open until 8:30. She hadn't taken time for breakfast, she was afraid to have anything on her stomach this morning. Besides, it was full already; jumping and growling at her, a thousand little worries marching through it.

Her intestinal revolt notwithstanding, Amy decided that a cup of coffee was necessary to steel her for the morning ahead. The sky was full of indecision; clouded, but lightening up here and there, never threatening rain but never promising sunshine. She glanced at the paper in her hand, not really reading it. The director of the daycare had handed it to her with apologies when she dropped her son off this morning and told her what it said. The facility was closing as of Friday and she would need to make other arrangements for her son. Amy placed the letter face down on the front seat of the car. There was enough to think about today. "This little stress with just have to wait its turn", she thought.

Ahead of her in the long line sat an ancient pick-up truck. It may have once been yellow but now had a myriad of colors, an unmatching red door, white primer over patches of "Bondo" and a bumper that seemed to consist mostly of rust. Every time the line moved forward, the driver had to start the engine which rumbled and shook the truck so that she thought it might just wiggle forward. When the line stopped moving, the truck shuddered and the engine sputtered and stalled out again.

On and on it went, the line moved often but not far at one time and the old truck would roar and rumble, shudder and shake until it sputtered another last breath. Amy found herself being more impatient than usual in the slow-moving line. It gave more time for the dread inside her to build to a crescendo.

The image of her ex-husband filled her mind. It was like him to force her back into court for no reason, filing ridiculous motion after ridiculous motion. Filing for reduction of child support he hadn't even bothered to pay in two months. Filing for visitation he knew the court could not allow. She prayed the court could not allow it anyway.

The line jerked forward again, finally the noisy truck and its stops and starts had passed the ordering station and had advanced around the corner to the pick-up window. Amy ordered just a small coffee and cursed herself for sitting in this long line for one item. She drove up to the window, getting out her wallet as she pulled up close to the uniformed man leaning out, her coffee in hand. She pulled a five dollar bill out and attempted to hand it to him.

"You're all set. It's all paid for", he announced, refusing her waving bill.

"What do you mean"? Amy asked him, feeling slightly confused.

"The guy in the truck ahead of you paid for your coffee". he answered. "He said to to charge him for whatever you ordered".

Amy just stared at him. The truck was just at the exit to the drive thru now, miraculously not stalled out. She wondered what he wanted.

The guy in the window kept talking. "He said to tell you, that you have everything a woman should have except a smile".

The words cut like a knife. Amy took the coffee and mumbled a "thank you". She noticed the truck just leaving the parking lot as she drove up to the exit. Suddenly she was suspicious and anxious. But as he drove off he headed to the onramp of the highway and continued on as she exited and went in the other direction.

She drove on into the day ahead, sipping her coffee and thinking about the strange generosity displayed by a unknown man in a truck that barely ran. Someone who gave something and wanted nothing in return. He could not know of the weight of life she carried. She thought about what he had said: "everything except a smile".

A slight shock of pain rippled through her chest as she thought of the stranger, who with only a few backward glances, was able to sum up her life in a cup of coffee.

Readers Response

Gone Away said, "That's it, don't tell me you've posted. I'm on the Rocket so I'll get off and come back and read. No time at the present, no time, no time!"

Ned said, "(Laugh out loud), the perfect comment. I haven't read this yet, but I wanted to say I will sometime..."

Gone Away said, " And I'm sorry I didn't stop to read straight away. This is wonderful, Ned. I think it's the best prose you've ever done. I love the way your poetic phrases are struggling through to illuminate the text with bright flashes of awareness. The writing is so good, so good. And the story is all you; it's excellent, marvellous, I can't think of enough adjectives to describe how good it is. And it's not just guilty conscience at my first comment - I mean this."

Ned said, "Thank you for such a nice comment. Although, I liked the first one too."

Glennie said, "What a wonderful story. I felt pathos, excitement, hope. the generous spirit of one who cared and yet wanted nothing in return. How does Amy feel now? Again I ask, when will you allow the public to read your prose."

Ned said, "Glenni, you are always too kind. This is the internet, how more public could I be?"

Andy said, "Great writing! Excellent story! You go to my blogroll, now."

Ned said, "Andy, so glad you stopped by and thank you so much for taking time to leave a comment. That always is appreciated. I will definitely check out your blog and thanks for the blogroll."

Harry said, "Zowie. What luck to discover there are two Neds who blob, and both do well."

Ned said, "They not only blob, they also bob and weave. It gets confusing when they pretend to be each other though."

Anonymous said, "Ned, as always, you leave me groping for words, because there's just no way to express how wonderful your writing is, or how deeply you can make me feel what you've written (unless, of course, I could write as well as you do. Which I don't). I once had a similar encounter with a stranger in a car when I was an impatient and aggressive teenage driver. I was following much too close, and literally bouncing up and down in my seat from impatience. With a simple patting hand motion, the driver in front of me indicated that I should take it easy...which made me really think about what I was doing to myself and those around me.

"Most people would have just used an obscene gesture, which would only have made it worse, but that one gesture transformed my driving habits and my thoughts about being on time. And that was 30 some-odd years ago."

Ned said, "That was a nice way to express it to you and most people would have used an obscene gesture or been angry. But most teenagers would have taken offense even at the nice gesture and would not have thought about their own behaviour, so it says a lot about you too. People are not always aware how they affect the lives of others, and may never know the good or ill they have done. Or how much a cup of coffee can really mean to someone."

The Village Idiot said, "Great story! Was it a dunkin donuts by chance? they line up out into the street for dunkin donuts coffee around here, so I figured it must be. I think they put crack in it. I'll bet the gal was especially glad since Dunkin Donuts coffee just went up by a dime a cup, at least at the one I go to. (though the price hike may have just been on the medium size, which wouldn't have had anything to do with the gal's small coffee).

"Good story, keep writing!"

Ned said, " Dunkin' Donuts is, of course, the finest coffee in the world and most certainly laced with mood altering substances. For further elucidation on the value of coffee, you can go here."

The Village Idiot said, "I Knew it!"

Anonymous said, "I once lived in a place where there were no Dunkin' Donuts stores. I don't live there anymore..."

Ned said, "In case of sudden removal from civilization (places where they have Dunkin Donuts) be assured that there is hope. Dunkins has a website and you can buy it online. Of course, you may have to provide an explanation of just why you moved away from Dunkins and it had better be a good one."

Jodie said, "Good to know, but I never, ever plan to live in such an uncivilized place ever again."

prying1 said, "Quite a nice story. Hoping it comes to memory in a timely manner as I need my attitude changed on occasion... - Thanks -"

The Preparation

The ground was thick with it, Nature's litter. Trees that once were plush green, had put on one last fiery show and shook off what they could no longer support. They settled for clean lines and a greyed minimalism; settled in for the grey austerity of a long winter.

"Autumn is not death" she said. "The sweet smell of decay. The forsaken leaves, the fallen, unwanted fruit. This is the preparation. It only seems final, because it may be our last chance."

Time ran on before us
It closed the day
It took our shadows
that had cast long ahead
I couldn't see where
We were going anymore

The snow came down slowly, silently, danced carelessly and without purpose. Each flake disappeared at contact with earth, succumbing to the warmth of its landing site. It was late October and the preparation was not complete. It comes back to me now. Each word strikes my memory as my feet strike the cold pavement and the echo of an uncertain gait returns to me from hollow streets. I wonder how many times I heard, not understanding?

She stood in the street
Her eyes were never upon me
The air was thick and white
Choking thick and white

Tornadoes swirled in doorways
Brown leaves dancing with the wind

"Winter symbolizes death" she said. "But if this were death, I would die readily. A death soft and pure. A death too beautiful for me."

I could only stand and look at her eyes, glacial and tearful. I wanted to know what she would not say; wanted to know that which she protected from my discovery.

What have you found in the garden?
(now sere and brown
the beds of summer's blooms
hard and dry)
What seeds of her sorrow
lie under this gathering blanket?

"Spring is not rebirth, only exhumation" she told me. "It is a falling away from grace, it is an unearthing. Beauty and serenity melt away. It is my death."

Love went on without us
It marched on through spring
She was gone from me
and I from her

Readers Response

glenni said, "What lovely symbols you have given us. I see a Monet depicitng the seasons and yet so much more. As the seasons prepare, would that we too could be prepared for 'life events.'"

Ned said, "It's the Boy Scout motto, Glenni. Be Prepared. Some thiings you can't prepare for though, can you?"

Mark said, "I especially love the word choices for each season, "decay," "death" and "exhumation." Some wonderfully descriptive sentences here Ned. Very enjoyable read, as always."

Ned said, "Mark, thank you. You always look into each piece like a writer, testing and tasting. It is good to have readers who feast on words."

garnet said, "Wow, powerful, dark mood. Exquisite setting and style. Sectioned pieces related like musical movements of a larger work. The ironic reversal of season's meanings is what really got me, though. This will stay with me."

Ned said, "Garnet, I really liked your reference to the movements of a musical composition. I hadn't thought of it quite that way, but the musician's perspective rings true. In a prose/poetry way, I suppose that is how it is meant to be read and heard. Thank you for your insightful comment."

splittinghairs (Janus) said, "Hard to follow up a great writing and good comments. I hope my lack of anything to say other than I liked it will be acceptable."

Ned said, "Janus, thanks. Your comments are always much more than just acceptable. They are well appreciated."

SilverMoon said, "Somber, heavy, cerebral and devastating. (I also liked those word choices for death already mentioned plus your brilliant use of irony regarding the seasons of time as you foreshadow the inevitable."

Ned said, "Silvermoon, I like it when people delve into the words and pull out emotions and moods. Thank you for allowing the poem to reach out. You're a great reader with a lot of insight."

Blueskytavern said, "I like the way you use words and construct these images and metaphors, Ned. This is sad, yet beautiful to read. I encourage people to read this out loud with emotion to experience the full effect of this."

Ned said, "Thank you Liz, that is truly a wonderful compliment. I like to be able to read aloud and I always hope people will read with emotion, whether aloud or silently."

Hereunder

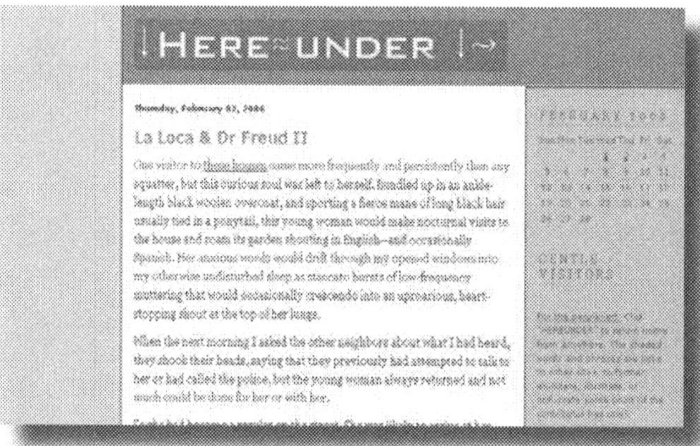

Hereunder is a blog I run with three other occasional writers, who are members of an informal writer's group. We rarely focus on the craft of writing, but instead post on various topics, using various genres (non-fiction, fiction, and poetry, and mixtures of these). All of the submissions above are my own.

Supposing You

Suppose that
Like the curd in your coffee cup–
The white, encurling speck
Arising from an unexpected
Turn of half-and-half,
And swelling on a brew of dark and rich
And flowing,
And with an ebbing flick of wrist
You toss him out.

Or.
Like the lint on your blouse's cuff–
The grey, enfibered jot
Emerging from a microscopic
Shift of weave and thread,
And clinging to a fold of dense and vast
And rolling,
And in a grazing pass of hand
You brush her off.

Suppose that
He or she supposed it–

This jot, this bright, ingrowing wight–
Supposing you, and every dream, or
Fear or idle thought,
Or smile or cough or hiccough,
Twitch or tic or tiny geste,
Were tossed out, brushed off,
Passed away.
Supposing you...

Readers Response

Gone Away said, "I'd comment but I'm durned if I'll be the only one again..."

Remainderman said, "Gone Away, if there were two Mozarts, two Bachs, two Michelangelos, or two DaVincis, then you might have a point. Comment away -- we always like to hear your thoughts."

Gone Away said, "Okay. Nice poem, I like the way it sneaks round to eventually point a finger at the reader and say, "How does it feel?" It may be that I am influenced by just having read another blogger, Matthew, and he is doing a series on abortion, but am I right in suspecting that there is an element of that subject in the poem?

"While on the subject of poems and comments, I have a friend who writes the most sublime poetry but she is a very private person and won't allow me to give out her blog address to anyone. I respect her wishes in that (although I itch to reveal her to the world - she is truly a world class poet - and I am not easily impressed) but I have taken the liberty of introducing her to your excellent blog. She has taken far too much note of your "rules" regarding comments and won't comment therefore, even though I assured her that she would not offend. I implore that you make clear to her (perhaps in a comment to this comment) that comments are truly welcome, as I feel sure you would enjoy her input - she is always clear, accurate and insightful in whatever she says. And I hope she blushes like a tomato when she reads this..."

"Thank you."

Remainderman said, "Yes. I was inspired by an old concept -- supposit -- that which underlies something in existence --- the subject. In today's language, it would be rendered something like the organic whole. Moreover, every visitor-- indeed, everyone in the world -- was once a tiny subject.

"We live for comments, and I would certainly welcome your friend's comments. In fact, I have just changed our welcome message: the prior message was unncessarily cute. See what power our faithful visitors have."

Gone Away said, "I am impressed and humbled by your willingness to accede to my request. Thank you again."

Remainderman said, "Just don't ask to change our editorial policies, because that would wrongly imply that we have any. By the way, where oh where is Harry?"

Gone Away said, "I would never ask you to change your editorial policies, existent or otherwise. As it is, I'm getting yelled at by my friend for having spoken to you about the commenting. Harry doesn't seem to have been around all evening. I suspect (although I dare not accuse him since I have no proof) that he is actually away doing something in reality, such as having a meal out or watching the television. There is a rumor going around that he is one of those folk who have a life! Not that I believe rumors, of course..."

Harry said, "Well, I will tell you fellows what. Eons ago, when I stumbled across art (and here I speak of canvas and paints and brushes), a co-worker asked the fair question, "What is art?"And so we came to our unschooled decision that art is something that evokes feelings, pure and simple. Good feelings, bad feelings; joy, fear or anger each qualified as equals -- if it moves one then yes, we agreed, it must be art.

"I still continue to think as innocently. Yes, and I am one of those who "knows very little about art, but he know what he likes". (there...I have forced myself to cliche, but it's late, so I forgive me) What I want to say here is that I must refuse any attempts to "explain" the thoughts of any artist, particularly when it comes to poetry, nor should I try. There are those much more qualified to speak on this -particular subject, such as Gone. (I seldom get poets at all. Nash is an exception. Silverstien is easy to me, and a hoot. But the deep things I recognize as being that, so I stay on the safe shore while I admire the glowing sun set or rise, and I keep my hands in my pockets as I breathe it all in. Ahhhh. How glorious!)

"Okay then. So Harry, how did it make you feel, reading this poem of Remaindermans?"

"Harry: Well, it made me think."

"Quizzer: About what?"

"H: You ask tough questions. Stop staring so hard."

"Q: Sorry."

"H: About life, mostly, and how damn unfair it can be. About people, and what shitheads they can be. Ya know."

"Q: Ah."

"H: Hey, don't "ah" me, pal. Yer not my shrink."

"Q: But..."

"H: Look. I liked it, all right?"

"Q: Gee, I simply wanted to..."

"H: AHEM."

"Q: Fine. I'll go, then. Let me get my things."

Gone Away said, "He does do great comments, doesn't he...?"

Ned said, "The poem is brilliantly done. It draws the reader in by way of a false assumption and begins to ask "how would you like it"? It lulls him into believing it is a call to more thoughtful and considerate behavior towards his fellow human beings then drops him into the realization that he, now considered a full-fledged human being, was once a tiny speck of as yet unspecialized cells, whose potential could not possibly be measured. Potential that is swept away because it is yet unseen, a speck that is as inconsequential and inconvenient as a piece of lint. Your blog was recommended to me by a friend whose good opinion is not easily earned. He did not mislead me when he told me that you have an excellent and well-written blog. I have enjoyed it and have added it to the list of blogs I read regularly. I would thank him, but he is Gone Away."

Harry said, "Ned's a fine mechanic, I see."

Remainderman said, "Ned, Thanks for your kind words. As for Harry, well, you should know that he has "issues" with mechanics."

Harry said, "Don't we all, until we discover the rare honest one."

Poor Relations: Himself's Near Death

Sure, Himself is down with the influenza.

Is that the way?

'Tis. He's been laying in bed half the week, sick as you like.

Ah, the creature!

Oh, now, don't be taking his part now, girl. Likely as not, it's mostly put on.

Oh, no.

See, now, he's got the whole lot of ya bamboozled. Sure, he's a great one for puttin it on, you know. There's the dishes waitin to be washed, and next thing he's got his feet up and cold cloth on his pate, swearing he's been struck with a fever. 'B'god' he says, 'this is it. I'm certain I'll die tonight. Run, now, and get the priest.'

And, I says, 'I'll not until you've got those plates scrubbed and put up.'

But, did he have a temperature?

Well, a course he did -- sure, we all do, don't we. His was a hundred three -- sure, just a few ticks above me own. And, him a man -- a sweaty and unruly man, at that -- sure, he's bound to be hotter.

But, no sooner had I taken the blessed termometer from his gob, he was up and sayin, 'Faith,' he says, 'Watch now, the merc'ry's ready to burst out an spill out on the floor an roll up in little balls. God save us.' With that, he fell back in the chair, as pale an brittle as me own mother's bone china.

But, sure, he must've been feverish?

Well, I don't know about that. Next thing he said he was chilled to the marrow, shakin and shiverin like a hindoo, and I says, 'Well, which is it? Hot or cold? Make up your mind. And, don't tink that first ting tomorrow, you won't be be up the roof tendin the hole ye made on Shrove Tuesday.' But, sure enough, that next mornin, I couldn't rouse him for nothin. So, I left him be.

Ah, the poor ting.

Not a bit of it. I'll have him up now scrubbing the floor in no time, and he'll be none the worse for it. I'm just after order'ing up his medications on the online apothecary.

Wonders never cease.

'Tis grand.

And, sure, he's still a fine figure of a man.

He is, at that.

Readers Response

Gone Away said, "Ah, she's a hard taskmaster, always with another job for the poor man. Almost as hard as this blogging business that takes no account of sickness or rest but says, "Get up, y' lazy thing. 'Tis bloggin' t' be done!""

Ned said, "While the sick man has life, there is hope. Be sure that it is not you that is mortal, but only your body. For that man whom your outward form reveals is not yourself; the spirit is the true self, not that physical figure which can be pointed out by your finger."

Marcus Tullius Cicero
Let us hope that this sickness, when defeated, will yet leave us a remainder of the man.

Remainderman said, "We are embarrassed by the wealth and versatility of our visitors: an Englishman who is an Irishman; a ned who is a poet and philosopher. Grateful we remain (thus the name)."

Gone Away said, "You are quite right Remainderman, both in regard to Ned and myself, for she is a poet of the highest calibre and I am from Coventry. My roots go deep into the past in the English Midlands, all of my ancestors originating from within twenty miles of that city, so I am as English as they come. But the Irish came in their droves to Coventry in the first half of the 20th Century, for it was the Detroit of Britain and there was work to be done.

I have worked alongside many an Irishman and enjoyed their friendship as well as their carefree philosophy and gentle, but oh, so witty, humor."

Harry said, "See, I get so jealous of ya'll, being raised mostly around Mexicans. None of ya prolly don't care much for hot sause, do yas?"

Ned said, "Harry, I love Mexican food and yearn for a nice picante sauce. None of this mild stuff for me. Luckily we have you to add spice to things."

Gone Away said, "In a survey conducted a few years ago, it was found that fish and chips was no longer the most popular take-out meal in Britain. That position is now held by the Indian curry, a state of affairs that I heartily approve of. My father having lived in India for many years before and during WWII, I appreciate a good curry and, contrary to the expectations of many, I like 'em hot enough to roast a Mexican."

Hannah said, "I have never tasted curry. Nachos, however, are on the owl-approved snacking list."

Remainderman said, "That does explain Harry's spice and bite."

Ned said, "Harry bites? Call Cesar Millan."

Harry said, "ARF! (this dog sits, but he don't beg)"

John Evans
Syntagma

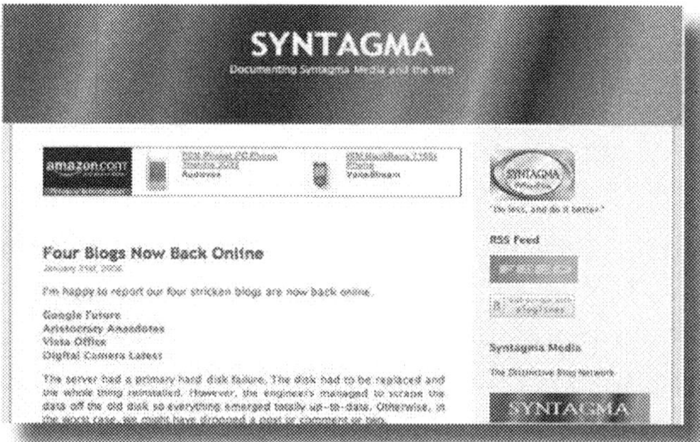

John M. Evans is an author, journalist, playwright and blogger who has been a full-time professional writer for ten years. John's published output is too numerous to list here, but his forthcoming nonfiction book, COSMOSITY, is due before Christmas 2006. John is the owner of Syntagma Media, a growing weblog network with a print publishing arm.

Surrogate Parent to an Orphan Seagull

Day 1

For my pains I've become a surrogate parent to an orphan seagull. The youthfully-fledged youngster landed in our ancient high-walled kitchen garden yesterday. As I'm temporarily here alone, the burden has fallen entirely on me.

The female chick (you can tell by the shape of the head), which is as big as an adult bird, can't yet fly, so probably fell off a rooftop and glided down into our patch. She keeps trying to fly up over the wall but can only manage a foot or two off the ground.

My first response was to leave the garden gate open in the hope she would find her way out. Alas, she viewed the opening with dark suspicion and eventually I closed it. It was time for Plan B.

The fact is, she's never going to survive out there in her present state of infancy. Her mother has clearly abandoned her as a lost cause and doesn't even come to feed her. A vet would say, leaving her to die might be the most "humane" course of action.

However, it occurred to me that if I could keep her alive for a few days, she might become strong enough to fly out under her own steam and find other gulls to protect her.

Yesterday, she had half my breakfast -- a bacon sandwich -- which she seemed to enjoy enormously. Hunger is a great leveler for a dainty palate. A tin of tuna fish went down well for lunch. I also discovered that if I leave the garden tap on slightly she will drink directly from the pipe.

She has also found a nest in a large pot with just a few weeds growing in it. I'm afraid the white mess splattered around the garden is not going to win me any friends, but I figure it can't be helped in the circumstances. She'll soon be gone and rain will wash it all away. This is England, after all.

She trusts me implicitly now, as I'm the one who delivers her food and obviously means her no harm. I'm hoping she doesn't imprint on me and imagine she's a human being. The good news is that every time birds land in the garden she imitates their flying action. I won't have to follow that chap in "Ring of Bright Water" and run around flapping my arms like a madman.

The poor thing has now injured her foot and is limping around the place like an invalid. The foot doesn't seem to be broken, just strained in some way. She won't let me touch it, though, and her razor-sharp beak is not something to treat lightly.

I've called her Rita. She doesn't yet answer to it though.

Day 2:

Well, what drama there's been here in rural Devon over the saga of Rita, the seagull chick. We're not used to such excitement out here in the sticks.

Last night, while it was still light, I heard a terrific commotion from our high-walled kitchen garden where she has been trapped for two days. Imagining a prowling tomcat dragging her away in his jaws, I rushed to her rescue. She was sitting as usual in the large pot she now calls "nest", and shrieking gull-like at the high-end of her vocal range. Her cosy position didn't suggest danger.

On the wall, about three yards away, stood a large, handsome, female herring gull, who was also giving vent to a torrent of gull-speak. Gulls never whisper. They always shout. They're like old Shakespearean actors, trying to make themselves heard at the rear of the stalls. Before this incident, I'd never heard a peep from Rita. That must be a good sign.

The obvious psychic bond between them suggested that this was Rita's mother. As soon as mum spotted me she majestically spread her surprisingly long wingspan and flew low and slow over the garden and away on the other side. Now, the fleeting glimpse I'd got of her eyes told me that she had noted the bowl of food, and the obvious good condition of her chick, and was satisfied that she was safe for the moment. After all, not many gulls get waiter service and bread fried in green olive oil. We are the swanky end of town.

It was clear that, in the conversation, something had passed between them. As soon as mom had gone, Rita popped out of her pot and started running up and down the garden -- despite her injured foot -- with her wings spread impressively wide. This was new behaviour and obviously came from the older bird. Don't tell me animals are stupid. Within the limits of their behaviour they're as intelligent as humans, sometimes more so. You'd never send a gull to Oxford, but we would never dive into the sea and come up with a fish between our teeth. On their own patch, birds are as bright as Albert Einstein.

There was still a problem though. Rita was now charging

full pelt, wings outstretched, up and down the garden. But in the middle sits a large, ungainly contraption which, paradoxically would make a good bird scarer. Not for our Rita though, she shot past it at speed time and time again. I was afraid she might hit the thing and break a wing. Now that would be a disaster. So out I went and shifted it to a corner where it wouldn't do any harm. Rita continued her frantic promenade until I left her for the night. And that was the conclusion of the evening's drama.

I was up bright and early this morning -- her third day in "captivity" -- armed with my new digital camera. As she has now become a Syntagma celebrity -- and they don't come any bigger than that -- a tasteful portfolio of photographs was a necessity.

Imagine my consternation on discovering she was nowhere in sight. I looked everywhere, under every tree and bush, in every slot and slit, fearing to find a bunch of feathers and the pawprints of a cat. But there was no sign of a struggle and nothing in the lane either. The bird had flown.

The canny older bird had probably returned in the early morning and guided her prodigal offspring up, up, and away, back to herring gull land, where the fish are fresher and the water dirtier than the stuff that comes out of my tap.

I have long known I would never make a press photographer. I always arrive too late.

The pity was I had missed my little chum's first flight, her flight to freedom and the bosom of her family. Do seagulls have bosoms? Never mind. Rita had triumphed over adversity, and I had played a small part in the drama by keeping her alive for two days.

When my own wanderer returns next week and she asks me the inevitable question : "How did you get on for a whole week without me?" I shall reply, as nonchalantly as I can: "Very well, darling, Rita kept me company."

Readers Response

The voluminous readers' response was lost when this blog was moved to a new domain.

Citations: How Academia Still Dominates the Web

Back in the dimly-remembered mists of the 1990s, the two mythical founders of Google, ~~Romulus and Remus~~ Larry Page and Sergey Brin, latched onto the citation system in academic publishing as a way of mapping and, ultimately, controlling the sprawling growth of the Internet. In many ways they could be compared to Capability Brown who turned wild nature into rolling parkland back in 18th-century England.

The legend has it that at Silicon Valley's Stanford University, Page saw literary citations as a software opportunity for the Web. Nowadays, it's hard to see beyond the system he produced: first BackRub, a way of measuring backlinks to articles and sites, and then PageRank, the most addictive element in Web one-upmanship. Has that system really served us well?

Academic books, monographs, and journal papers have become vast collections of citations. Many books are now almost unreadable, since their sole purpose is to show off the reading of the author. University contracts stipulate that dons, lecturers and professors must publish regularly on their subject or face isolation and career meltdown. The necessity to publish or be damned has driven down the quality of academic publishing for years.

Compare and contrast an academic book on a specific topic with the trade-publishing equivalent written by a competent professional author. There really is no comparison on quality, readability, range and breadth of aspiration. Authors trounce academics every time.

Many academic tomes are just webs of citations. Why, though, are we better served by knowing what hundreds of other people have written, rather than the authors themselves? Many citations point to arguments absorbed from other sources in any case. So we're taken round in circles within the discipline covered.

Thanks to Google, the Web now has the same problem. To gain Googlejuice you have to cite and cite regularly and relevantly. The blogosphere, in particular, is a madhouse of clickability. Click, click, clickety-click it rattles on day and night, a cacophonous syncopation counterpointing the melody from Google's cash tills.

The genius of Google is that it didn't just transfer the bane of academic publishing onto the Web, but that it discovered how it could profit enormously from the process.

Will the next big entrant — the Google of the future — take us away from the Groves of Academe to a less cluttered way of measuring our worth and relevance? Or is the interconnectivity of the blogosphere in particular, the very essence of what it is?

Readers Response

As this was a new blog when this was posted, there was no posted response.

Karin Goers
Phillywriters

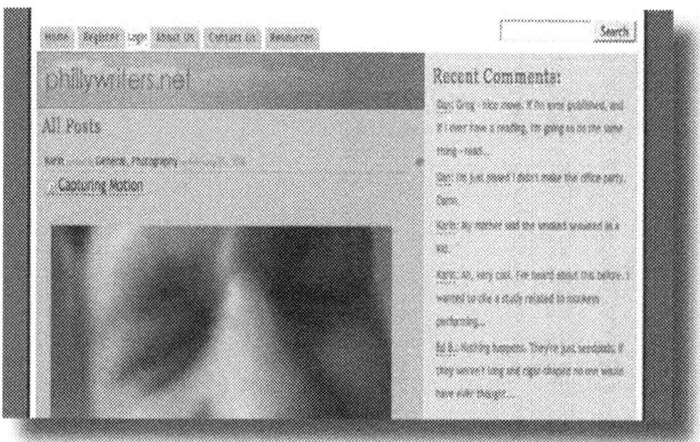

I am fiction writer living in Philadelphia who makes a living as a software developer. I am the co-founder of the writers community, phillywriters.net, as well as the sole contributor to the blog 'The Thumbless Wonder'.

My Blogs

http://thumblesswonder.blogspot.com/
http://phillywriters.net/

Capturing Motion

I've posted the pictures from Rebecca's office party.

When I first showed them to Rebecca, she said something deep about how these pictures capture the essence of motion — the idea that everything is constantly moving, even down to the most infinitesimal degree.

I said, "Really? Cool! I thought I was just drunk."

Readers Response

Rebecca said, "Uh, uh. What I said was — maybe humans interpret another being's motion subconsciously. These blurry pictures somehow capture the essence of that motion — and that's why they are so pleasing — because they reveal some hidden truth about people. Except for the one where Schiller has a head growing out of the side of his face."

Karin said, "Oh. I like that even better. Sorry I didn't remember. Now that you said it again I remember. Didn't I say I was wasted?

"Whoa! This is trippy. I think you're addressing how, in social situations, you intepret other people consciously, subconsciously, and unconsciously, which is why social situations can be so challenging and stress-inducing (which is probably why we resort to substances).And it's probably why we can very quickly determine whether we like someone or not. (Very Malcom Gladwell, no?) And this is what you were saying to me when we were sitting on the table. Duh.

"But what I initially said is true, too — albeit less sophisticated — which is why I like taking pictures of people when they don't expect it, and especially when they're trying to resist it. So… in addition to exposing potential hidden truths, the multi-faceted nature of individual expression is also revealed.

"We all have trouble seeing pictures of ourselves. Our mind's eye projects an idea of What We Look Like. Photos are very disturbing because they challenge that idea.

"Sometimes I think people would rather walk through life with a placard that covers their faces and displays their best photo. Candid photos expose the weird physical flaws we'd rather pretend don't exist. They remind us those flaws are indeed on display for the world to see.

"What we don't realize is that the world doesn't see our flaws how we see them. Look at that picture of Russ. Obviously, it's not his most flattering angle. But doesn't it capture the essence of his spirit? I think it does. I think he looks lovely.

"I haven't yet accepted this myself. One of the perks of being the photographer is that I can choose which photos make it beyond the cutting room floor, and which ones don't. The ones where I look like a big fat blurry blob didn't make it."

ThinkingManatee said, *"'Maybe humans interpret another being's motion subconsciously.'*

"That makes me think of mirror neurons, which allow us to have a subjective experience of other people's actions when we see them moving.

http://en.wikipedia.org/wiki/Mirror_neurons

"I like to imagine what kind of role mirror neurons play in art. It's been shown that they fire off when you read a novel. I think they fire almost as strongly when you read about somebody eating as they do when you watch someone eating. (I think they also help you to interpret what somebody is going to do next.) Very cool research."

Karin said, "Ah, very cool. I've heard about this before. I wanted to cite a study related to monkeys performing non-sensical, group-induced behavior even though the sensical option was available to them — but I can't find it.

"The mirror neuron wiki passage links to Theory of Mind information, which I read about when we had the conversation about consciousness awhile back (pre-server-crash days).

This theory of mind covers two separate concepts:

1. Gaining the understanding that others also have minds, with different and separate beliefs, desires, mental states, and intentions

2. Being able to form operational hypotheses (theories), or mental models, with a degree of accuracy, as to what those beliefs, desires, mental states, and intentions are.

"I find this interesting with respect to Rebecca's initial comment. To me, it suggests that in a social environment, we consistently look for clues from others that reveal their particular "state of mind". And it's through passing judgment on a given individual's "state of mind" — or on a group's — that we select a "state of mind" for ourselves that is complimentary to the individual or the group at hand. Or a contrary one, depending on the circumstances.

"Then, if Person A behaves in a manner inconsistent with Person B's perception of Person A's "state of mind", then dissonance occurs in Person B, which likely resutls in the deployment of various defense mechanisms.

"(God, that last paragraph sounds so technical.)"

Dan said, "I'm just pissed I didn't make the office party. Damn."

Ernesto Banawa
Peripatetic Mind

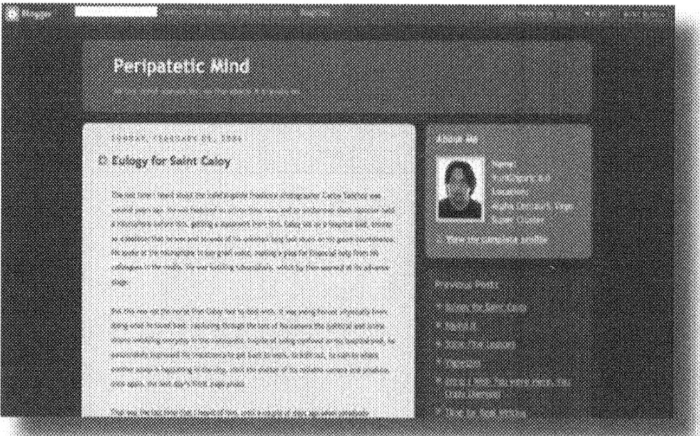

My post Goodbye Ruby Tuesday (Friday Nov. 4, 2005) gained a response not from a lot of readers, but from the very person the blog post was intended to. Most of the times, it helps when a good number of readers get to comment and applaud your for what you have posted. But there is nothing like a reaction from the very person you intended the post to be, since it drives the purpose of posting point blank at its subject.

Speed-reading the Subterraneans

A typical scenario where a reader is swept by the magical power of a book and considers it as one of his favorites is purchasing a title (learned and heard from a friend or those people he reads) from a bookstore. He then relish its content, probably with his feet prop up on a coffee table.

But then, there are other ways that can spice up the reading experience where the reader and the book get a complete concentrated connection, thus creating a memorable reading nirvana. The potency of the book itself strikes him like a battering ram straight to the marrow of his soul and the experience does not just come from the text itself, but also from the events surrounding him when he devours every written word of the book.

What can be a more extremely exhilirating experience than trying to finish a book amid a bombardment in a time of war, and the knowledge that any moment a bomb can end your life abruptly without reaching the last page? Well, that is far from my story. Nevertheless, I like to think of it that way.

With just enough money for fare on my way home (my broods just dropped me on the mall on their way to my parent's house as the night descended), I went straight to the bookstore to do some "free" reading, oblivious to the fact that I looked like a ragged bum in pair of borrowed sandals, hundred-peso t-shirt, and fading black shorts.

I could have picked Italo Calvino's titles from the bookshelves if there were no Kerouac titles that caught my fancy. I was then just recently acquainted with the literature of the Beat Generation, having read Jack Kerouac Big Sur and Dharma Bums and been salivating for a copy of On the Road (which I have to read until this day since it seems to disappear on bookstores the moment it hits the shelves).

What I found was just more than a hundred pages of a book titled Subterraneans, which according to the blurb, Kerouac wrote in marathon typewriter-yakking for three days and three nights. And probably he wrote that in an inebriated frenzy.

I picked a vacant chair and proceeded to devour the book with a resolution to read it in one sitting. What is a more apt way to read a three-day frenzied labor of typewriter-yakking than finishing it in one sitting with an estimated highway speed that can make your hair recede from the strong winds of printed words slapping your face and your brain. That resolution also stemmed from lack of dough and to avoid reading a book in weekly installments, which I know would slow down the momentum of the story and with me expectedly forgetting what the book is all about.

I breathed in a lungful of oxygen then promptly submerged myself in the ocean of reality of the post-war American literature of the Beat Generation.

The book is a narration of a bohemian writer Leo Percepeid, about the history of his breakup with a Negro girl named Mardou Fox, a member of an intellectual group called Subterraneans.

Here Kerouac wrote again about the free-spirited, amoral culture of the Beat Generation in search for an identity along their pursuit of artistic goals: be successful writers and poets. It was the time of bob jazz, never ending boozing and arguments about literary subjects. It was the time when the post-war children of America were growing up.

Amid this wayward culture of "tea" smoking, casual sex, teenage angst and rebellion to be left alone by the authorities, still, deep longing for love could blossom. But the twist is that that was an era when everybody was leeching each other.

By the time I submerged myself again into the book (seeing those sitting around me changed faces and I looking at the staff of the bookstore, wondering if they would approach and tell me: "Sir, there is a minimum quota of hours for reading a certain book for free. If you want to continue reading, go find another book), a Yugoslavian young poet by the name of Yuri Gligoric has already surfaced in the story.

I again zipped in the rollercoaster/talkfest/speed-typing text set by Kerouac on Leo and Mardou's bohemian love affair. And before I knew it, getting all weary in the eyes and the bookstore's well-lighted interior blurred before me, I failed to notice that I was up for a heart-wrenching ending as I reached the last several pages.

And there happened the tragic breakup of Leo Percepeid and Mardou Fox because of Yuri Gligoric. This is a 20th century fiction that can hit any reader's heart with the hip word: "Well, baby we made it together," with Mardou Fox telling Leo Percepeid casually about what happened to her and Yuri.

The jeepney I rode going home sped on South Super Highway with me still seeing visions of printed words on darkened factories, of the 50's America, of the Beat Generation, of Leo, Mardou and Yuri. And that hip word "made it" reverberating in my ears. My head was throbbing. I needed to pound on my PC to release this neverending yakking in my head. And now, finally, I write this.

Note: This appeared on *The Philippine Star* on November 9, 2003 as the week's winning essay in My Favorite Book Contest. I posted it here since I could still recall the rush I felt when I first read the book.

Deborah Woehr
Personal Journal of a Writer & Artist

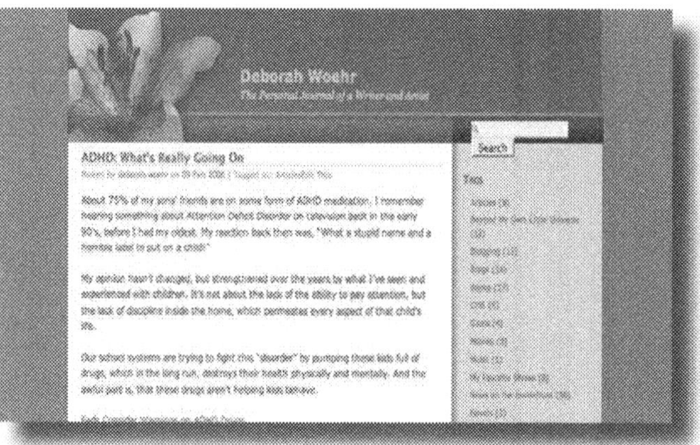

Deborah Woehr has been writing horror fiction since 1997. She founded *The Writers Buzz* in 2004, with the aim to help promote the works of new and established writers. In 2005, she co-founded the *Writer's Blog Alliance* with fellow blogger, Clive Allen. She uses her personal blog to buzz her upcoming novel, express opinions about issues that are important to her, and to have fun.

ADHD: What's Really Going On

About 75% of my sons' friends are on some form of ADHD medication. I remember hearing something about Attention Deficit Disorder on television back in the early 90's, before I had my oldest. My reaction back then was, "What a stupid name and a horrible label to put on a child!"

My opinion hasn't changed, but strengthened over the years by what I've seen and experienced with children. It's not about the lack of the ability to pay attention, but the lack of discipline inside the home, which permeates every aspect of that child's life.

Our school systems are trying to fight this "disorder" by pumping these kids full of drugs, which in the long run, destroys their health physically and mentally. And the awful part is, that these drugs aren't helping kids behave.

Readers Response

fredcq said, "I agree with you 100%. I'm not sure what is going on with today's kids but where are all this is coming from. I agree with your assessment of "lack of discipline" but let me also throw something else out there. Diet. My fiends think that their son is ADHD because he is so hyperactive. They are great parents overall but they let the kid have tons of sugar. I have seen him drinking coke and eating cookies all the time. No wonder he is running around like a nut. I also think that kids sitting in front of a TV all causes them to have attention problems. Either way, I don't think that pumping them full of drugs is the answer."

Karen Lee Field said, "Whilst there may be some children with a real problem, I believe most are undisciplined little brats. In other words, I agree with you. When I was young, we used to play outside for hours, these days I rarely see kids in the street. What are they doing? Watching TV, playing PlayStation (or it's equivalent), or messing around on the computer. No wonder they have so much energy to burn.

"Also, parents don't have control of their children like the "olden days". New laws are to blame for this, most of the time. The parent isn't allowed to discipline their children and can be charged with "child abuse" for simply smacking their child for misbehaving (it never did me any harm; the couple of times it happened to me).

"Our world is going down the drain…fast. I hate to think of what the future generations will be like, and to be honest I don't think I'd have children in today's world (if I was just starting out)."

Lee said, "I also agree. Kids seem to have the run of the house these days and I think a lot of it is the parent's fault. No one wants to play the bad guy and discipline the little shit. But it has to be done. The world is already filled with lazy parents, or money hungry parents, and the kids get to do what they want. Imagine what the future will be like if this continues. Drugging the kids is NOT the answer."

pat kirby said, "Totally agree. Although I don't know if all are undisciplined brats. Many are, granted. But today's school systems, with regimentalized curricula are a poor match for many young boys (the most often diagnosed as ADD). Interesting article in Newsweek recently about boys and how they learn. Basically, "boys will be boys" and expecting them to act like girls is asinine.

"One problem I see, is that the media has blown up issues like child abduction to such an extent that parents won't let their children play outside–Ye ole, "stranger danger" B.S. (Contrary to the media's misdirection, most kidnappings and abuse are committed by friends and family). Also, in the quest for "safety," kids aren't allowed to be kids. (Pain is part of the necessary landscape of growing up.)

"Kids don't blow off any steam or get any exercise."

Deborah said, "Fred, I'd forgotten about the diet issue, but it is so true. My son's best friend is the only one who has true ADHD, and his mother figured out that he couldn't have foods with a particular red dye. Caffeine and sugar are other no-no's for him."

"I agree, Karen. Society has gone way overboard in the opposite direction, claiming that kids are "little adults" and that we should treat them as such. Whoever invented that term needs to look up "adult" in the dictionary.

"A swift swat on the butt does not equal child abuse. Sometimes it's necessary if the child gets out of control to the point where he/she is going to hurt themselves or somebody else. But the media and the social workers have gotten everyone hysterical over this issue."

fredcq said, "I don't even think that my friends son is ADHD. I think that he is just loaded up on sugar. I have seen him be fine and then running around like a loon after soda and cookies." Sorry, I had more to say. (grin)

"We never give our daughter sweets. We don't even really keep junk food in the house. When she is at my mother's house, they sneak her all kinds of cookies and stuff. We can see the change in her behavior after an afternoon with them.

She speeds around all over the place. I have gotten to the point where I have to monitor everything that they give her!"

Deborah said, "I agree with you on the lacksadaisical parenting, Lee. Your job as a parent is supposed to be focused on discipline and building a moral and ethical foundation, not being their "buddy." I'm grateful that I've met a group of parents who share the same values.

"My sons' teachers always tell me how good they are, which makes me feel proud as a parent. But I feel bad for the other kids, who unless they figure out how stupid Mom and Dad are, will be lost."

(to fred's last comment) "Oh, yes. The grandparents! "Spoil them and send them home," my father-in law used to say."

"Pat, my boys are bored to death with the school curriculum, which is so outdated it isn't even funny. You made a great point about boys being expected to behave like girls. My husband and I discussed this about 8 years ago and believe it's true. The school system is trying to turn our sons into docile little mama's boys. Can you imagine these kids growing up to be soldiers? I can't.

"As for the media hyping up "stranger danger," I wish that was hype for our neighborhood. Our old house was a block away from the elementary school, but we didn't dare let our kids walk by themselves because of the problems with vagrants, most of whom were insane. Three girls were accosted within a six-month period. In our new neighborhood, we let our kids ride their bikes up and down the street. But they're always alert to the crazy drivers."

Lee Pletzers said, "When I was teaching Karate in NZ, one of the kids was ADHD according to his mother and everyone else. He used to run around licking the floor and many other things and it was impossible to get him to do anything. Usually he was okay, but sometimes he was off the wall hyper and I learned that sometimes he would eat tonnes of sugar straight from the packet, whenever mum and dad weren't looking."

michaelm said, "I'm with you as well, Deb. I've said time and time again that most behavioral problems regarding children stem from the home. As they say, "the apple doesn't fall far from the tree," and I truly believe that to be true. It seems it's always one step forward, two steps back. If it doesn't work, medicate it. Sheesh..."

Deborah said, "Lee: As a co-leader for my oldest's Cub Scout den, I found that these kids hard enough to deal with. Michael: Their parents were even worse."

Marti said, "I think you have made a very valid point... I was a room mother for years, and many of the "hyper" kids just wanted someone to pay attention to them! Often the parents both worked out of the home, the kids watched endless hours of TV and video games (alone), getting little exercise or interaction with their parents. Great post- thanks for sharing!"

Deborah said, " Hi, Marti, Thank you for sharing your experience. I know exactly what you're saying about the attention factor. I was also a room mother, but for a year. This one little girl kept stroking my hair and trying to sit on my lap until I had to gently coax her into working on the assignment that her group was working on. I talked to the teacher about what to do, and she said that this little girl was a handful. Yes, I agreed. But I also remembered what my mother-in-law had told me once. Negative attention is better than no attention."

Traditional vs. Online Education

Quoted from Some Students Prefer Classes Online (Yahoo! News)

"In fact, the distinction between online and "face-to-face" courses is blurring rapidly. Many if not most traditional classes now use online components — message boards, chat rooms, electronic filing of papers. Students can increasingly "attend" lectures by downloading a video or a podcast."

One of the arguments presented in the article were the motivations of the students. Some are too lazy (or hung over) to get out of bed and go to class, yes. But there are the rest, who either can't get into a required class because it's full or don't have time during the day because they work.

I've taken classes traditionally, online, and through correspondence. The latter two methods weren't any more difficult academic-wise. However, there were days where I had to force myself to sit down and complete an assignment. Self-discipline and motivation are key components to succeeding with the distant learning method.

The one thing I liked the best about distant learning was that I can go at my own pace. There were some subjects that I zoomed through, while others needed more time and attention. There are some subjects that I would rather take in a traditional classroom. Math has always been my worst subject, for instance. If you were forced to change careers and needed a degree, which route would you take?

Readers Response

Benjamin Solah said, "I'm currently studying via correspondence, and I must say, it is not my thing. It is partly getting motivated to do the work, partly the fact that there is much more enjoyment in learning with other people personally, and part the fact that the course is crap. My teacher barely knows how to respond to an email. The assignments are pointless (almost all consisting of 200 word essays. 200 words!) I better get into Sydney Uni because I'm not continuing with this."

Cavan said, "You can lump me in with the "lazy" group. At my school, you need a machete to cut through all the red tape involved in signing up for distance ed classes, so I go the traditional route. Of course, being lazy, I don't always make it to class. The other university in town has its own local TV channel and most of the classes are broadcast on it. So, a lot of students stay home and simply tape each class. I'd love a setup like that, but I guess I'll have to stick with waiting at the bus stop in the cold Canadian mornings for the time being."

Deborah said, "I don't envy those cold Canadian mornings or the long, boring lectures. (grin)"

Lee Pletzers said, "I'm into online classes, basically 'cause I work all day and most of the evening and have a limited time frame to get things done."

pat kirby said, "For a real degree–as opposed to some of the fluffy stuff that certain "get your degree in a year" outfits offer–I'd go the traditional route. I've taken online classes for work related training. Invariably, I lost motivation and got bored. When possible, I just cheated.

"I need a teacher and the motivation that comes from dragging my butt to class. Also, I enjoy the interaction with other students.I don't know what I'd do if I had to go to school now, though. I just can't imagine mustering the motivation or interest."

Deborah said, "Lee: I went to a tradeschool at night, after working 10-hour days. It's tough. If I had to do it all over again, I may opt for the online education.

Pat: There's a lot to be said for social interaction. Some courses require it. As for the online degrees, I found it prudent to investigate the school to find out whether or not their curriculum was on the up-and-up."

Fredcq said, "If I was going to go back to school, I would loathe having to sit in class again, lol. I would surely go the online way."

Marti said, "I like online learning as well. Being able to set my own pace was the biggest advantage. Good discussion!"

www.ingramcontent.com/pod-product-compliance
Lightning Source LLC
Chambersburg PA
CBHW051231050326
40689CB00007B/876

* 9 7 8 1 4 3 0 3 0 9 2 9 1 *